CUBS ON

No sooner [...]
overgrown g[...]
back again. [...]
   'Here,' he [...] secret.'
He looked a[...] sure no one was
watching them, then he whispered. 'The loot
is buried in the garden. Now don't tell the
police, the master criminal is in police headquarters. Remember my words, the loot is in
the garden!'

CUBS ON SATURDAY

Stephen Andrews

Illustrated by Val Biro

Beaver Books

A Beaver Book

Published by Arrow Books Limited
17-21 Conway Street, London W1P 6JD

An imprint of the Hutchinson Publishing Group

London Melbourne Sydney Auckland
Johannesburg and agencies throughout
the world

First published by Hodder & Stoughton 1976
Second impression 1983
Beaver edition 1985

Printed and bound in Great Britain by
Anchor Brendon Limited, Tiptree, Essex

ISBN 0 09 941970 X

Contents

1 · The secret of Nat's plot

AKELA stood before his Cubs of the 2nd Billington Cub Scout Pack. He looked at his watch. For a moment he seemed confused, which was unusual, for he was seldom uncertain of what to do on Cub nights. The trouble was, it was too early for flag-down, and too late to start anything new. Akela waited for complete silence. The Cubs, squatting in a circle around him, stopped their shuffling, and listened.

'Think of a word,' said Akela, 'the name of an object, any object.'

Georgie White, the Tawny Brown Sixer, better known to his pals as 'Snowy', looked out of the window at the rain.

'Umbrella!' he said.

'Right, umbrella,' said Akela. 'Another word.'

'Bun,' said Podge, always thinking of his stomach. During their break, Akela had let them have cheese buns with their lemonade.

'Right, bun,' said Akela.

'Banjo!' said another Cub.

'Banjo?' echoed Akela.

'Nelephant!' yelled little Christopher Clark, a freckle-faced youth with sticky-out ears, known to all as 'Nobby'.

'Nelephant? Right, thanks, enough, enough,' said Akela. 'Umbrella, bun, banjo, nelephant. I remember the games my old Scoutmaster used to get us to play. One of them was to give us half a dozen words, and then ask us to tell a little story using those words. Let's see if my rusty old brain is still working. Umbrella, bun, banjo, nelephant . . .'

Akela paused. The Cubs watched him in silence.

'This afternoon,' went on Akela, 'I took my umbrella to Belle Vue zoo as it was raining. There I saw a nelephant called Joe. I said, "Hello, could you eat a bun, Joe?" To which the nelephant replied, "I'm so hungry I could eat a banjo!"'

The story was received in stony silence, then suddenly Nobby burst out laughing.

'What a rotten story,' he roared, and rolled over on his side, creased with laughter. 'Can . . . can you eat a bun, Joe!'

At that, the rest of the Cubs burst into laughter, not at Akela's silly story, but at Nobby's helplessness, and before long, thirty-odd Cubs were rolling about the floor, just as helpless.

'If it's not funny, don't laugh,' said Akela, but this only made the Cubs laugh even more.

'I . . . I can eat a banjo,' wailed Nobby, tears streaming down his face.

This set the Cubs laughing again, and it was fully two minutes before Akela could begin to make himself heard.

'The story may not be funny,' said Akela, 'but making it up does require brain effort. As I said, my old Scoutmaster was very fond of giving us brain teasers. Another thing he was very fond of was the initiative exercise, that's like a brain teaser, where you do something. You see, you are all growing boys, babies no longer. Your parents and teachers are spending less time looking after you. One day you'll have to face the world and stand on your own two feet. Initiative exercises are useful because they exercise your common sense. When I think of a few, I'll try them out on you. Since Nobby finds it so funny, he can try the first initiative exercise, with Snowy, his Sixer.'

Akela scribbled a note on his pad.

'Your exercise is this . . .' He went on to read from his note. 'From the gate, proceed north until you see red, turn left to a place of learning, look for a pin, proceed on your way without turning, go through the world's smallest jungle, bang the fox's head three times, and ask the first man who speaks to you for his autograph.'

'Eh?' said Nobby. 'Will you say all that again, please?'

'No, I will not!' said Akela. 'I've written it all down on paper.' Akela tore the top sheet from his notepad and handed it to Nobby. 'That should keep you out of trouble tomorrow. Tell us how you get on next week.'

'Goo!' said Nobby, goggling at the paper, as Snowy looked over his shoulder. 'I don't fancy banging a fox's head three times . . . Can't we just stroke a little pussy, or something tame. . .?'

Akela ignored him, and looked at his watch. His little talk on brain teasers and initiative exercises had nicely rounded off the evening. He clapped his hands.

'Who is the Duty Sixer? You, Bobbie? Your turn to lower the flag. Cubs, form circle.'

Snowy was just a little dazed by the turn of events. He could hardly wait until the next morning, when he and Nobby would tackle the strange task Akela had set them.

On Saturday morning, Snowy and Nobby met at the gate of their Cub Headquarters. Snowy always had a holiday feeling when he was out on Saturdays. Of all the days of the week, Snowy liked Saturday best. He liked Friday evening, for that was Cub night, but Saturday could almost be called Cub day, for Akela usually had something special arranged. Today, it was an initiative exercise. Snowy had never done an initiative exercise before, and he did not know how it would turn out. He felt he was about to start a great adventure.

'This must be the starting point,' said Snowy. 'I can't imagine what other gate Akela meant. Let me look at the instructions again, Nobby.'

Nobby showed him the paper.

'From the gate, proceed north . . . that's that way. Come on, Nobby. We must proceed north until we see red.'

'There's a fire-station round the back,' said Nobby.

'But that's not to the north, and it's not red, is it? The fire-engines are white now, anyway, so they can be seen in the dark. Ah, look!' Snowy pointed ahead to a set of traffic lights.

'That's green,' said Nobby, but just as the words were out of his mouth, the lights changed. 'Red, I said.'

'This must be it.' The Cubs walked up to the traffic lights. 'So we turn left to a place of learning . . .'

'We can't do that!' said Nobby.

'Why not?' asked Snowy.

''Cos the lights have turned green again.'

'Oh, come on. We've got to find a place of learning next.'

Snowy looked ahead and saw a school. 'There's a school, Nobby.'

'It's . . . it's a girls' school,' said Nobby.

'Well, it's a place of learning, isn't it?'

'It is, I suppose, if you call knitting, hockey, screaming, yapping and whatever else they do in there . . .'

'Well, I won't argue about that,' said Snowy. The Cubs came up to the school entrance. Snowy looked at the paper for the next instruction. 'Look for a pin,' he read out. 'A pin?'

'A pin? I've got one in my shirt,' said Nobby, lifting up his jersey, 'It's a safety pin where a shirt button used to be. A safety pin is a pin. This will do, won't it?'

'Don't think we'd come all this way just to see a safety pin in your shirt,' said Snowy. 'Anyway, what's the next instruction? Proceed on your way without turning. Proceed on your way? But which way is our way?'

Snowy looked around. His eye caught the name of the street opposite.

'Pinview Crescent,' he said. 'Pinview! Look for a pin – Pinview!'

'Eh?' said Nobby.

'We go straight ahead, down Pinview Crescent. Proceed on your way without turning.'

'You can't go straight down there without turning,' said Nobby. 'It bends round the corner, like a banana.'

But Snowy was sure of himself. He raced on ahead into Pinview Crescent.

'Look,' he said. 'There's a public footpath ahead. We can go on, without turning.'

Nobby looked down the footpath. 'Coo, I haven't been down here before.'

The narrow footpath was screened on one side by tall hawthorn hedging. On the other side was a row of small back gardens, which were kept by their owners in various states of untidiness. Most of them had a few rows of vegetables, some had patches of lawn, one even had a garden pond with a few plastic gnomes dotted about. Of the dozen tiny gardens, only one could be said to be well-kept, but that was beautiful.

'I haven't been down here before, either,' said Snowy. 'I think Akela lives around here somewhere, doesn't he? I wouldn't be surprised if these instructions lead us to his house, and he's the one we have to ask for his autograph.'

'What a rotten trick,' said Nobby. 'If he wanted us to have his autograph, he could have given it to us last night, instead of getting us to tramp out here, wasting shoe-leather.'

'Look for the world's smallest jungle,' read out Snowy. 'The world's smallest jungle! I wonder where that can be?'

Snowy looked over the low hedges at the back gardens. What first caught his eye was the beautiful garden with a neatly trimmed lawn, and a spick and span greenhouse, on the back of the house, full of

healthy plants. But the next garden, by complete contrast, was knee high in weeds. It had just been left to run wild.

'The world's smallest jungle?' Snowy asked himself, but there was no doubt in his mind. He looked at the house. On the back door was a big iron knocker, shaped like a fox's head. 'Knock on the fox's head three times,' said Snowy, opening the gate. 'This is it, Nobby, but if this is Akela's garden, I'm surprised he leaves it so untidy.'

'So am I,' said Nobby. 'And he's always telling us to be neat and tidy. The next time he tells me to get my hair cut, I'll tell him to get his garden cut.'

'Give me a lift up to the knocker,' said Snowy.

Nobby knelt down on the doorstep and Snowy climbed on his back and banged the knocker three times. Snowy climbed down to wait for a reply.

'Here,' said Nobby, frowning as he straightened up. 'I hope Akela didn't bring us right out here to dig his garden.'

'Get down on your hands and knees on the doorstep and I'll knock again.'

No sooner had Nobby got down on his hands and knees, than the door opened. Out came a very old man, crooked, with a nobbly stick.

'Who are you? What do you want?' said the old man, poking Nobby in the ribs with his stick. 'I don't want to buy any tickets, or have any jobs done. Clear off!'

Nobby scampered away and hid behind Snowy.

'We . . . we only want your autograph,' said Snowy, holding out a book and pen.

'Autograph?' said the crooked old man. 'He, he, he! How did you know I was famous? You clever boys. Come in, come in.'

The crooked old man turned back into the house. Snowy followed him cautiously, with Nobby clutching at the back of his jersey.

'Do you . . . do you think it's safe?' whispered Nobby in Snowy's ear.

'Akela wouldn't send us anywhere not safe.'

'I don't know about that. Akela said he'd like to string me from the top of the flagpole, and that's not safe.'

'Ssh!' said Snowy.

'Ah, this is my room', said the crooked old man. 'Come in, come in.'

The two Cubs were ushered into a small dark and dingy room. The furniture, that is a table, chair, roll-top desk and bookcases were little better than those found in junk shops. The place was full of dusty old books and magazines, stacked here, there and every-where. There were even a couple of volumes on the floor, propping up a leg of the rickety old table. The room had the appearance of a second-rate, second-hand bookshop.

'Fancy you two knowing I was famous,' said the old man. 'A light on a hill is difficult to hide.'

Nobby looked around at the stacks of books.

'Goo, did you forget to take your books back to the library?'

'Oh, these? He, he, he! No, these are mine. This is where I do all my research.'

'Research?' said Snowy, not seeing anything at all scientific about the crooked old man.

'Yes. Oh . . .'

Nobby accidentally trod on the books propping up the leg of the table.

'You dropped some books on the floor,' he said.

He bent down to pick up the two books which propped up the leg of the table. The table tilted, and the ink-pot on top, rolled across in a great arc.

'The ink-pot!' cried out Snowy, unable to reach it, but he levelled the table as best he could.

'I've got your books,' said Nobby.

Nobby stood up and bumped his head on the bottom of the table. The table top tilted the other way in spite of Snowy's efforts to keep it level, and the ink-pot jumped off into the old man's hands. It was a good catch, even if the ink-pot was upside down. The old man put the messy ink-pot on a sturdy pile of

books and waved his inky fingers at Nobby.

'You horrible little boy,' said the crooked old man, clawing at the air in front of Nobby's face. 'Come to make my life a misery, eh?'

Nobby hid behind Snowy.

'It . . . it was an accident,' said Snowy. 'We only want to collect your autograph, then we'll be off.'

'Ah, my autograph,' said the man, still clawing at the air with his inky fingers. 'Yes, yes, I can see you are clever boys.' The old man took a couple of letters from his roll-top desk and wiped his hands on them. 'Publishers' letters, bah! Now then, my autograph. Would you prefer me to autograph "The Home-grown Potato"?'

'You can't write on a potato,' said Nobby, 'can you?'

'No, no, no. I mean my latest book – "The Home-grown Potato". I wrote it, as you well know.'

'I've never read it,' said Nobby, but the man ignored him.

'If you would prefer me to sign your autograph book, I'm not one to complain.' The man signed Snowy's autograph book – 'Nathaniel Stone – Author.'

'Now, my next book, "African Jamboree" for instance,' he went on, 'is about this jamboree for Scouts in Africa. But . . . he, he, he! I'm not telling you the story. If you want to know that, you'll have to buy it when it comes out. All I have to do is find a publisher.'

'I'll . . . I'll add it to my reading list,' said Snowy.

The man shook an inky hand with them.

'Remember, if you want another autograph, don't be afraid to come and ask for one, and tell all your pals to do the same.'

'Thank you, I shall,' said Snowy. 'Goodbye!'

'Goodbye!' said the man.

'Where's the door?' said Nobby.

'I'll show you. Don't trip over the furniture. Are you always clumsy, boy, or only when you come to see me?'

No sooner had the Cubs reached the wild, overgrown garden, than the man called them back again.

'Here,' he said. 'Let me tell you a secret.' He looked around to make sure no one was watching them, then he whispered. 'The loot is buried in the garden. Now don't tell the police, the master criminal is in police headquarters. Remember my words, the loot is in the garden!'

'What loot?' said Nobby.

'What loot?' echoed the man. 'Er . . . the town hall silver.'

'You mean the town hall silver which was stolen last summer?' said Snowy. He remembered the newspaper reports he had read of the theft, which was still an unsolved crime. 'The police haven't caught the burglars yet . . .'

The man put his finger to his lips. 'Ssh! Don't tell the police,' he whispered. With that, he went inside and slammed the door.

'What . . . what does he mean?' said Nobby, shuffling out of the gate as fast as he could. 'The loot is in the garden! Hey, Snowy, you don't think he's a criminal, do you? He was itching to get his hands around my throat, you saw that.'

The Cubs hid behind the thick hedge and peered into the overgrown garden.

'I don't know what to think,' said Snowy. 'The stolen town hall silver never was recovered, was it?

We'll have to tell someone about this. We'll have to tell the police.'

'We can't do that!' shrieked Nobby. 'He said . . . the master criminal is in police headquarters . . .'

'We can telephone the Manchester or Stockport police,' said Snowy. 'There can't be a master criminal in every police station. Come on, let's telephone the police.'

They found a public telephone box in Pinview Crescent, just opposite the narrow footpath. The Cubs squeezed inside, but instead of dialling 999, which would connect them to the local police station, they looked up the number of Manchester Police headquarters in the telephone directory. Snowy lifted the telephone from its cradle and dialled that number.

'Manchester Police headquarters,' said a voice. 'Can I help you?'

'Yes, er,' said Snowy. 'I'd like to report an unusual occurrence. A man has just told us he has loot buried in his garden.'

'Loot?'

'The town hall silver . . . '

'Keep talking. I'm listening . . .'

The police sergeant listened to Snowy's story, then asked lots of questions, names, addresses and about everything that happened.

'Now I want you to stay where you are,' said the police sergeant.

'Billington is outside our patrol car area, but we've got a C.I.D. detective-inspector who is handling this case. I'll get him to come to you immediately.'

Snowy put down the telephone. 'Let's keep our eyes on the suspect until help arrives,' he said.

The two Cub Scouts crept down the narrow foot-path, making the best use of the cover provided by the hedges. They were interrupted by a shout from above.

'Hey, Snowy, Nobby!'

The Cubs turned and saw the smiling face of Akela, peering down from the upstair's window of the neatly painted house.

'Did you get your autograph?'

Snowy stood up. 'Autograph? Oh, yes.'

'Let me see it,' said Akela. 'I'll be right down.'

Akela withdrew his head and closed the window. He came to meet them at his back gate.

'How did you get on?'

'We got his autograph,' said Snowy, 'but . . .'

'He's a criminal,' said Nobby. 'He's got loot buried in his garden!'

Akela laughed. 'He was my old Scoutmaster. He's a bit crusty now, but in his day, he was one of the best . . .'

'He said . . .' said Snowy, 'he said there's loot buried in the garden. We telephoned the police . . .'

'You did what?' echoed Akela.

'He said there's loot buried in the garden, the town hall silver, but we mustn't tell the police because the master criminal is in police headquarters. We had to tell someone. We telephoned Manchester police. They're sending a detective . . .'

'They're what?' groaned Akela.

'What else should we have done? said Snowy, desperately. 'Do you expect us to forget the whole thing?'

'Oh, no, no, no, no, no,' said Akela. 'In the circumstances, from what you tell me, you did right. But I wonder what the old codger's up to now?'

Surprisingly enough, the plain-clothes policemen arrived within half-an-hour, which was very quick indeed, considering the distance they had to come from the big city. A man introduced himself as a detective-inspector of the C.I.D. He had a burly young assistant. Akela ushered them through his back garden into his lean-to greenhouse.

'Come in, gentlemen,' said Akela. 'You can see the next door garden from my place, and you will also have time to consider the case before you make any hasty arrests.'

'I've been investigating this case for months now,'

said the detective. 'That silver is very valuable, you know, some of it goes back to the reign of Charles II . . .'

'But you don't really expect it to be hidden in the garden next door, do you?' said Akela. 'He's . . . he's my old Scoutmaster.'

The detective looked out of the greenhouse window at the overgrown garden.

'The loot could be there,' he muttered. 'I have known stranger cases. It's my job to investigate this case by following up every lead there is until the case is solved. This is the best lead I've had for months.'

The detective-inspector asked the Cubs to repeat their story, and all the time they were talking, he looked out of the greenhouse window at the overgrown garden. Finally he grunted.

'We'll have to see about this!' he said. 'Come on, Joe.'

With that, he and his assistant went next door.

'Whew!' said Akela. 'I'd hate to be a silver burglar with those two bloodhounds on my heels. They never give up, do they!'

The detective-inspector banged on the fox's head knocker. Akela opened a little window in his greenhouse, so he could hear, as well as see, what went on next door. For a while, there was no reply to the in-

spector's impatient knocking, then the door creaked open and a face peered out.

'Not today, thank you,' came a croaky voice.

The door was about to close again, when the detective-inspector put his foot in the door.

'Mr Stone?' he said. 'I'm Detective-Inspector Ashford, C.I.D. I'm making enquiries about the loot said to be buried in your garden.'

'What loot?' said Mr Stone.

'The town hall silver . . .'

'Ah, that. It's a long story. I didn't want the police to know about it, really.'

'Oh, didn't you?' said the detective-inspector. He nodded at his assistant who walked away back down the footpath towards Pinview Crescent.

'Since we are here, perhaps you will be good enough to show us just where the loot is.'

'There isn't really any loot,' said Mr Stone. 'I . . . I

deliberately told the Cubs not to contact the police.'

The detective's assistant returned from his car wearing gum-boots. He was prepared, with a digging fork and pickaxe.

'We can't take any chances, Joe,' said the detective. 'Give it a good going over.' The detective turned to Mr Stone. 'Perhaps you will give me a statement, sir. Inside the house if you don't mind.'

The detective and Mr Stone went inside the house. Joe probed around the tiny garden, sliced off the tops of the weeds and probed some more. He started digging where he expected to find the missing town hall silver. Working systematically, he combed the whole patch. It was only a tiny garden, but he was soon covered with perspiration. Finally he stood up and mopped his brow.

'There's no town hall silver here,' he cried. He called inside the house. 'I've gone all over the garden, but I can't find any trace of the loot.'

The detective-inspector and Mr Stone came out.

'I told you there was no loot,' said the author. 'You see, I'm writing a book about loot in a garden, and to find out people's reactions, I told a couple of Cub Scouts, that there was loot buried in my garden.'

'The next time you get an idea for a book, keep it to yourself, otherwise I'll have you arrested for wasting police time.'

'Don't worry,' said the author. 'I have all the material I need for my new book now.' The plain-clothes policeman walked away down the footpath towards their car. 'Thank you for your help,' the author called after them. 'I'll send you all a free copy of my book when it's published – autographed!'

The detectives disappeared from view.

'Good riddance,' said the author, as he walked back.

Akela opened his window wider. 'Hey, Nat! Where did you really hide the loot?'

The author looked up. 'I tell you there's no loot. The police ought not to have come.'

'Another of your brain teasers misfired, eh? You can't blame my Cubs for that. They did their duty. Had you really been a criminal, you would have been locked up by now.'

'Bah!' said the author angrily.

'Well, you have got the information you need for your book,' said Akela.

Nobby stood on the seat so his head was level with the open window.

'Yeah!' he said, 'and you've got your garden dug over for free – all ready for your home-grown potatoes.'

2 · Book worm

Of course, when Snowy and Nobby recounted their initiative exercise adventure, at the next Cub night, every Cub present wanted to try one.

'All right, all right, all right!' shouted Akela above the noise. 'Quiet, everybody, quiet!' He waited for the noise to subside. 'I have plenty of initiative exercises for everybody. Indeed, life itself is full of initiative exercises. Everything you do is an initiative exercise. Every problem is an initiative exercise, so don't run away from them. Use your common sense and see them through, and you'll find life is an adventure. As far as the last initiative exercise went, Nobby and Snowy tackled it very well indeed, and I hope the potential author got the material he wanted for his books.'

Akela frowned for a moment. 'Talking of authors and books,' he went on, 'how many of you are in a library? Put up your hands those of you who have joined a library.'

About half of the Cubs put up their hands. Nobby put up his hand, pulled it down, put it up again, pulled it down and half put it up.

'Are you in a library or aren't you?' snapped Akela.

'I don't know,' said Nobby, meekly.

'What do you mean, you don't know? You must know! Even you must know that.'

'I've got a ticket,' said Nobby, brightly.

'If you've got a ticket,' said Akela, slowly and deliberately, 'why don't you get yourself a book?'

'I did have a book once. You see, when I joined the library, I got a big, thick book with lots of pictures and reading and writing in it, all about different countries and people and stories and things.'

'You mean an encyclopædia,' prompted Akela.

'No, it was a book, with real pages in it,' said Nobby seriously, 'and after I'd finished with it, I took it back to the library, but the lady wouldn't take it back. She said it wasn't theirs.'

'You didn't take it back to a different library, did you?' asked Akela.

'Oh, no I wouldn't do that,' said Nobby. 'I took it back to the same library, but the lady looked through all the tickets in her trays and couldn't find mine. She asked me when I got the book, and I said before dinner. Then she said she hadn't had her dinner yet, and I couldn't change the book the same morning, and she chased me out and she said if I could read a big, thick book in ten minutes, I could read it again.'

Akela sat down on a chair, utterly confused.

'So you haven't got a ticket, you've got a book, right?'

'No, I've got a ticket,' said Nobby. 'I forgot I had the book, for weeks and weeks, might have been years, then the library lady sent me a postcard saying, "Where's my book?" or something like that. So I took the book back to the library, and you know what? She charged me five pence for not bringing back the book earlier, and I hadn't even read it properly.'

'So you've got your ticket!' Akela smiled.

'Yes,' said Nobby, 'if it isn't out of date. It cost me five pence.'

'And you never went back for another book?'

Nobby shook his head.

'Ah!' Akela sighed, and looked over Nobby's head at the rest of his Cubs. 'Nobby still surprises me, even when he runs true to form. But what surprises me even more is that half of the Pack are not in a library. Ah, you don't know the pleasures you are missing. Books . . . ah, we'd be so poor without them. Show me a boy who has not enjoyed a book, and I'll show you a prize ignoramus.'

Nobby tried to hide himself behind his woggle.

'Next Friday, I want to talk to you about libraries

and books,' went on Akela, 'and I want you to talk to me about some of the library books you've read and enjoyed. Now, before I forget, if any of you are planning a trip to the library, go along tomorrow, because the library will be closed early next week for spring cleaning. More about that later, Now I think it's time for a game. We'll start with British Bulldog. Red, Green and Grey Sixes versus Blue, Yellow and Tawny Brown Sixes . . .'

The Cubs charged to take up their usual positions at either side of the hall. Snowy nudged Nobby.

'Hey, Nobby. There's something about book reading in the Cub Scout Handbook. How about going to the library tomorrow to see what they've got?'

Nobby frowned. 'All right, Snow. Good idea.'

The next morning, Snowy called for Nobby to go to the local library. Nobby was gloomy.

'I was up nearly all night trying to find my ticket, but I found it,' said Nobby, holding up a yellow ticket 'It was out of date last week!'

'Never mind, Nobby, you can change it. Come on, Nobby.'

'Are you sure, Snowy?'

'Yes, come on.'

The Cubs were early and got into the library just after it opened.

One of the lady librarians was drawing a little

picture on a note-pad with a ball-point pen.

'Have you changed the date on the date stamp, Valerie?' asked a stoutish lady, the chief librarian.

'Yes,' said Valerie, finishing off her doodle.

Nobby looked over the counter. 'Have you got any books?'

Valerie rolled her eyes. 'Well, we don't sell fish. What sort of books do you want?'

'What sort of books do you have?'

Valerie rolled her eyes again. 'Everything! You mention it, we've got something on it.'

'Have you got any colouring books?'

'No, we haven't' said Valerie.

'But you said you've got all sorts of – '

'My friend's ticket is out of date,' butted in Snowy. 'Can he have a new ticket today?'

'Go on through. I'll have it ready for you next time.'

Snowy gave Nobby a push through the swing gate. He handed Valerie his book and she gave him his ticket, then he went through the swing gate to join Nobby in the library. Nobby saw a pair of library steps and climbed up them.

'Goo, what little stairs,' he said. 'They've only got two steps and they don't go anywhere.'

'Come down.' said Snowy. 'They're to reach the high shelves in the adult library.'

Nobby jumped down and looked about him. 'What a lot of books. You'd have to have a big head to read all these.'

'Ssh!' said Valerie. 'No noise in the library, please.'

Nobby tip-toed round the bookcases to the children's, section, as quietly as a Red Indian on the warpath.

'What sort of book do you want, Snowy?' he whispered.

'Oh, I don't know yet. Anything interesting. Hey, here's a book on Scouting – oh, I think I'll have this.'

'There aren't any other books about Scouting, are there?'

'No . . . o, but you can borrow this when I've read it.'

'Oh, thanks, Snowy.' Nobby resumed prowling round the bookcases.

'Here's a book about uniforms, if you're interested.' said Snowy, taking a red covered book from the end of the shelf.

'Where, where?' said Nobby. 'I like uniforms.'

Nobby grabbed the book, opened it up and beamed at the full-colour illustrations.

'This is a good book,' he said. 'I think I'll have it.'

'Here's a book about badges,' said Snowy, pulling out a book with a gaily coloured jacket.

'I like badges,' said Nobby. He slipped the red book back in its place at the end of the shelf and took the other book from Snowy. 'You certainly know how to find good books, Snowy.'

Nobby glanced at the pictures of the badges, then he put the book back, and took out the book on uniforms. He glanced again at the pictures of the uniforms, and swapped the books around again.

'I don't know which book to take out,' he said, for the third time taking out the red covered book. 'I like badges, and I like uniforms, and I want to read a book and tell Akela all about it next Friday.'

Snowy shrugged his shoulders. 'Take one today, and the other one another time.'

'But I don't know which book to take out today,' Nobby whined. Again he swapped books.

At this time, Valerie, the young librarian, was replacing returned books on their shelves in the adult library, in the next room. There, the top shelves were rather high, so she used the two-step library ladder. Snowy wandered away with his book under his arm.

'Which book would you choose if you were me, Snowy?' called Nobby.

'Which book do you think Akela would like me to show him?'

Valerie leaned back on her ladder.

'Ssh!' she said. 'No talking in the libr—'

Suddenly she screamed, overbalanced, dropped the pile of books she was holding and fell awkwardly to hit her head on the floor. Snowy rushed to assist her, to help her up, but found she had knocked herself out cold. Nobby came to see what was the matter, and behind him, the chief librarian.

'Get out of the way,' said the chief librarian.

'I didn't do it, honest,' said Nobby.

'Give her air, give her air,' said the chief librarian, as Snowy raised her head.

Almost immediately, Valerie opened her eyes and groaned. She rubbed her head.

'Ooh,' she groaned. 'My head!'

'Take it easy,' said Snowy.

Valerie seemed all right, although her face was quite pale.

'I'm . . . I'm all right now, thank you,' she said.

'Come and sit down,' said the chief librarian, escorting her to the staff room.

Snowy picked up the scattered books and piled them on top of the library steps, then he went along to the staff room in case he should be needed.

'Try some deep breathing for a moment,' said the chief librarian. Valerie breathed deeply at the open window for a few moments.

'I'm all right now, really I am,' she said.

'I think you'd better take the rest of the day off.'

'No, I'm all right, truly, besides, Saturday is our busiest day.'

'I'll manage, dear. Don't worry about that. You've had a very nasty knock, so you can't be feeling too well. It's better to be safe than sorry. You can take it easy for the rest of the day at home.'

'We'll see she gets home safely,' said Snowy. 'Akela, our Cub Scout Leader, told us in a first aid talk that if anyone is knocked out and recovers, we must still see him safely home, in case it's serious.'

'It's not serious, really . . .' said Valerie.

'Nevertheless, you do look pale,' said the chief librarian. 'That's a good idea. These boys can see you home. I'll get your coat.'

The chief librarian waved away Valerie's protests and got her coat from the cloakroom.

'This is awfully nice of you,' said Valerie, as she was helped on with her coat. 'I only live round the corner.'

'Nevertheless, you'd better let the boys escort you home.'

'It's no trouble for us,' said Snowy. 'I'll take out this book if you don't mind.'

The chief librarian stamped Snowy's Scouting book.

'Oh,' said Nobby. 'I haven't got a book yet.' He dashed back to the book shelves and grabbed the red covered book from the end of the shelf. 'I'll have this one, please.'

Nobby's book was stamped, and the Cubs, one on either side of Valerie, escorted her out of the library.

'This is awfully kind of you,' said Valerie again. 'I only live round the corner, and I'm feeling much better now.'

'Well, it's on our way home,' said Snowy.

Valerie smiled. 'I'm happy to see Cub Scouts are chivalrous, like knights in shining armour. What's your book?'

'Oh, it's about Scouting,' said Snowy. 'Akela, our Cub Scout Leader, said he would like us to show him our books next Cub night.'

'I've got a book about uniforms,' said Nobby. 'I saw another book I liked about badges, but I can borrow that another time.'

'Oh, you like badges?' said Valerie.

'Oh, yeah,' said Nobby, 'especially Cub Scout badges. I like collecting badges. I haven't got any yet, but I hope to start collecting. I'm hoping to get my Bronze Arrow next year.'

'Oh, I have some badges you can have.'

'Have you really?' said Nobby. 'Have you got any Bronze Arrows?'

Valerie turned down a little alley. 'I live here. If you wait a moment, I'll get the badges for you.'

The Cubs waited while Valerie went inside her little house. In a moment she returned with three cloth badges. She looked at the Cubs.

'You've got plenty of badges on your jersey,' she said to Snowy, 'so you won't mind if I let your friend have these, will you?'

Snowy shook his head. 'Not at all, miss.'

Snowy had a dozen badges on his jersey, including his Gold Arrow and Sixer Badge. Valerie gave the badges to Nobby.

'Oh, thanks,' said Nobby.

'You are sure you are feeling well now?' asked Snowy.

'Yes, thank you. I'll be back to normal after I've had a cup of tea. Thank you for seeing me home.'

'Good. Cheerio,' said Snowy, turning to leave.

' 'Bye!' said Valerie, closing the door.

'Aren't these badges super?' said Nobby, as they walked along the pavement.

Snowy nodded.

Suddenly Nobby frowned. 'What are they? Oh, no, they're Brownie badges!'

'They are still badges, aren't they?' said Snowy, uneasily.

'But . . . but I don't want to collect Brownie badges!'

Nobby sulked along. They passed a grocer's shop with a pram parked outside. In the pram was a baby, playing with a rattle.

'Here!' said Nobby, throwing the badges in the pram. 'Sew them on your nappy.'

Nobby walked on, with his hands in his pockets.

'Brownie badges, huh!'

Snowy shrugged his shoulders. 'Never mind,

Nobby, you've got a good book to show Akela on
Friday night, haven't you?'

Nobby brightened. 'Oh, yes,' he said. 'I'm going to
read this book through and through, every night next
week and tell Akela all about it.' He opened the book.
'Oh, no!' he groaned. 'Oh, no! I've . . . I've taken out
the wrong book.'

Snowy looked over his shoulder.

'What have you got?' he asked. 'What's it about?'

'Dress-making!' groaned Nobby.

3 · Bee in his bonnet

Snowy did not read his Scouting book that week. He did not want to have an interesting subject to talk about at the next Cub night, when his pal, Nobby, had nothing but the hands in his pockets. Nobby violently refused to return his dress-making book to the library that same day, and even resented any mention of the subject. The library was to be closed for the first three days of the next week, and that, Nobby felt, would not leave him sufficient time to read and prepare a suitable talk for Akela. Snowy said he had lots of other books which Nobby could borrow. But, as Nobby said, Akela had specifically asked them to use their library books, and he would talk about the subject no further.

In spite of that, the Cubs' talk on library books turned out to be a huge success. This was almost entirely due to a new Cub in Red Six, little 'Woody' Knott. He had a book about bees, and he told everyone what he had discovered about bees, how they built their hives, how they lived and how they made honey.

Bees made honey by bringing up half digested food from their stomachs. That was honey. Many of the Cubs had no idea that was how bees made honey. Nobby didn't even know bees made honey.

'I didn't know bees made honey,' said Nobby.

'Then who do you think makes honey?' asked Akela.

'The Co-op factory!' said Nobby.

'Well, now you know something you didn't know before, don't you?' said Akela.

'Yes,' said Nobby, thoughtfully, then he put up his hand. 'Do wasps make marmalade?'

'They do not,' said Akela, sharply. 'Marmalade was first made out of oranges and other ingredients for a French king who had an illness. The French for "my illness" is "ma maladie" from which we get the word marmalade. Anyway the king was cured, and everybody wanted to try this marvellous stuff called marmalade. Do you see?'

Nobby looked blank, but in spite of that, everyone in the hall, even Akela himself, had learnt something he had not known before. Snowy had been surprised to learn that a bee could communicate with its fellow bees, and tell them the whereabouts of food by dancing in a special way.

'I'll bring in a pot of honey next week,' said Akela, 'then you can all try a dollop of the real stuff. I shall also be interested to hear if any of you have discovered anything new about bees. We'll have another talk on the subject as part of our nature study programme.'

The talk had certainly set Snowy thinking about bees.

'Let me remind you,' went on Akela, 'next Saturday is the day of the Scouts' spring fête, and I want all you who have volunteered to help, to be here by ten o'clock tomorrow morning to help build some of the stalls and games. Even if you don't intend to be on a stall, your help will still be appreciated. There's a whole pile of bunting and flags to sort out besides a bit of painting to be done . . .'

Snowy and Nobby had planned to run a little film show at the spring fête, and they intended to turn up the next morning to prepare a room for their show. But so interesting had been little Woody Knott's talk on bees, that Snowy could not get the thought of them out of his mind.

'There's a man who keeps bees in his garden just behind the fire-station,' he said to Nobby. 'He should be able to tell us about his bees, if we ask him politely.'

'He might give us a pot of honey,' said Nobby. 'I like honey.'

'He's usually in his garden on Saturday mornings.

Let's pop round and see him tomorrow morning, before ten o'clock. I'll give you a call, shall I?'

'Right, Snowy. Give me a call about nine.'

The next morning, Snowy and Nobby made an early start. They cut down a path by the side of the fire-station to the bee-keeper's place. Snowy led the way.

He was half-way down the path, when a swarm of bees, like a big black cloud, swirled towards him. Snowy stood perfectly still. Then the biggest bee he had ever seen, flew on to his shoulder, and crawled beneath his scarf. At once the rest of the swarm settled on him. He was covered, literally from head to toe, with the crawling insects. He was as black as if he had just crawled out of a vat of tar.

'Don't touch me,' said Snowy, standing perfectly still, and speaking through half-closed lips. He knew that if he should try to disturb the bees, or injure any in any way, they would sting him. 'Don't touch me.'

'Jump in a river,' shouted Nobby. 'Jump in a river.'

But soon Nobby had his own worries. Three of the bees buzzed around his head, and Nobby danced about, yelling in horror and swiping out in all directions with his cap. When a bee came too close, Nobby dropped his cap, raced back down the path, and jumped into the safety of a telephone box. There he felt a little relieved, until he noticed a little pane of

glass was missing from one side. Having nothing at hand to plug the gap, he stood with the seat of his trousers against the opening, hoping the bees would not see that as a likely target.

When, at last, Nobby saw that his bees had gone, he plucked up his courage to put his mouth to the opening.

'There're no bees in here, Snowy,' he yelled. 'Come in here and you'll be all right.'

But Snowy was still covered with the crawling insects. What worried him was that if the queen bee was making a nest under his scarf, the swarm would never go away. As it was, they were crawling all over his face and neck, arms and legs. And surely, if he should unfasten his scarf, and by doing so, injure the queen bee, the swarm, in their fury, were likely to sting him to death.

Out of half-closed eyes, Snowy saw the bees crawling over his nose and cheeks. He saw the bulky pollen bags on their legs, their composite eyes, the hairs on their backs, their waving antennae, their long tongues and the barbs of their stings. Beyond that, in the background he saw a man running towards him. He was the bee-keeper.

'Keep still, sonny,' he said firmly. 'Don't move.' The man looked all over Snowy. 'Funny! I can't see the queen bee.'

'I . . .I think it's under my scarf, at the back,' said Snowy, without moving his mouth. 'That's where the largest bee settled.'

The bee-keeper went behind Snowy and fumbled under his collar.

'Ah, got her,' he said.

He appeared, holding a large bee between his finger and thumb and boldly walked off with it. The swarm rose and flew off in a cloud after him. Snowy heaved a sigh of relief. The bees had left him, every one, and he had not a mark on him.

A woman cautiously looked over the hedge.

'Are you all right, boy?' she asked. 'We saw you set upon by that swarm of bees. I sent my daughter to fetch the bee-keeper. I keep telling him he shouldn't keep bees in the neighbourhood, where they can sting people, but he never listens. All he says is they won't sting you, unless you hurt them, but I know they do. I've been stung myself three times already. People shouldn't be allowed to make a nuisance of themselves like that. We are living in fear.'

'Thank you for sending for help,' said Snowy. 'I don't know what I would have done had he not got them away.'

'Well, don't you go down the path any farther,' said the woman. 'That bee-keeper has some more down there. They'd sting him if he wasn't so thick-skinned.'

The woman snorted, shuffled back down her garden path in her slippers and went back into her house. Snowy scratched his head, then he looked around for Nobby. He saw Nobby creeping sheepishly down the path.

'Have they gone yet?' Nobby whispered, picking up his cap.

Snowy nodded. 'There's nothing to worry about. They won't sting unless you hurt them. Let's go and see how the bee-keeper is coping.'

'No, no, no!' whelped Nobby.

Snowy looked up, surprised that Nobby should be afraid of bees. Nobby shrugged his shoulders.

'All right, then, only for a little peep,' said Nobby.

The Cub Scouts then cautiously proceeded farther down the path, to where the bee-keeper had his garden. They found him putting the lid on one of his bee-hives. The boys watched from outside the fence.

'Ah,' said the bee-keeper. 'This is my lucky day. It's not every day I find a swarm of bees. Very valuable, they are, should produce quite a few kilos of honey.'

'Have you got them all in that box?' asked Nobby.

'Yes, they've all settled down in their new home. Do you want to see them?'

'Yes, please.'

'No, thanks.'

'They won't hurt you.'

'I don't trust them,' said Nobby. 'They may not like me.'

Snowy was more trusting than Nobby, and he went into the garden for a closer look at the bees.

'They must have mistaken you for a shrub in that green jersey of yours,' said the bee-keeper, good-humouredly. 'They didn't hurt you, did they?'

'Not at all.'

'Of course they don't,' said the bee-keeper. 'Yet I'm always getting complaints these days. Some folk complain if they see a bee within ten metres. Don't they know bees fertilise their flowers?'

Snowy nodded. He was surprised to see how quickly the new swarm had settled down. Already some of them were out, scouting for pollen. One of the bees was in the entrance of the hive, fanning away with its wings to provide a simple but effective form of ventilation.

'Have you kept bees long?' asked Snowy.

'Ha!' laughed the bee-keeper. 'All my life. My grandfather kept bees on this very site before me. I reckon bees have been in our family for well nigh a hundred years. But since these houses have been built, people have never stopped complaining. They don't want bees, but they want the honey. If I could afford to, I'd pack up and move away into the country.'

Snowy could see both points of view. Town folk, in their ignorance, were honestly afraid of bees, and bee-keepers were being put out of business by the spreading towns.

'I owe it to you for capturing that swarm,' said the bee-keeper. 'Let me give you a pot of honey before you go.'

The bee-keeper went off to his shed. Snowy followed him, and was presented with a little earthenware pot of honey.

'Oh, thank you,' said Snowy.

'Good stuff, that,' said the bee-keeper. 'Pure honey,

not this artificial stuff. I wish I had the space to make more.'

'Couldn't you start up a bee farm in the country?' said Snowy, not really knowing the problems involved.

'A bee farm?' said the bee-keeper. 'I wanted to do that twenty years ago, but I couldn't afford it. You need money for that sort of thing. I had thought of the idea before, but it would have been a struggle to make ends meet.'

'If people want honey, someone must produce it for them.'

'Um!' said the bee-keeper. Suddenly his appearance

changed, as if he had just thought of something. 'Um, I might be able to raise the money now. Come to think of it, I should get a good price for what I've left of this land. Land prices for building have rocketted up these last two years, and with an advance on my pension, which I'm entitled to . . .'

'It would solve a couple of problems, your's and theirs.

'Place in the country again,' he murmered. 'I . . . I could grow a field of flowers as a side-line. As well as producing pollen for the bees, they would produce seeds.' The bee-keeper snapped back to reality. 'You've put an idea back into my head, sonny. You've made me feel an old fool for not seeing it myself, but you've given me a new lease of life.'

The bee-keeper went out into the garden and sat on a garden bench.

'I can look out for a bit of land at weekends. If I sell up here, give up my job at the fire-station . . . A bee farm in the country!'

The bee-keeper had forgotten all about Snowy, but Snowy did not mind. He left the old man dreaming, and went off to see how the bees were getting on. Suddenly he heard a yell from behind the hedge. Nobby had discovered a bee buzzing around his head and immediately began swiping at it with his cap. The bee dodged the wild swings and actually landed on Nobby's hair. At this, Nobby let out another yell, and raced away as fast as he could go.

Snowy followed. He saw Nobby run as far as the main road and turn right by the telephone box. Then he went on, past Cub Headquarters and up to the stone bridge which spanned the stream. Before Snowy could stop him, Nobby vaulted onto the stone parapet and leapt into the stream.

Snowy hurried to give his assistance, but he was beaten by Akela who had come out of Cub Headquarters to see what was going on.

'What's . . . what's up with him?' said Akela.

Nobby was sitting in no more than fifteen centimetres of water. He cupped his hands together, scooped up as much water as he could hold, and splashed it over his head.

'What's . . . what's he trying to do, have a bath with his clothes on?' said Akela, as Nobby continued to splash himself vigorously.

'You could say he's got a bee in his bonnet,' said Snowy.

Akela glared at Nobby sitting in the shallow water.

'Looks to me as if he's got ants in his pants,' he said.

4 · Friday night fry-up

When Snowy offered to share his pot of honey with the rest of the Cubs, Akela thought it would be a good idea if they all had a camp-type feast on their next Cub night. He contacted his Sixers personally and asked them to pass on the word to the Cubs in their Sixes. Every Cub was to bring a knife, fork, mug and a couple of sausages for a Friday night fry-up. On the expected night, he lined up his Cubs and inspected the outstretched hands of each Cub in turn.

'You'll do,' he said to Snowy. He passed on down the line until he came to Nobby. 'What have you been doing with your dirty little paws, mining coal?'

Nobby looked at his hands. 'I've . . . I've only been greasing my bike. You are always telling me to keep it well oiled and greased.'

Akela nearly exploded. 'But I didn't tell you to grease your fingers, did I? Oh, Nobby, you'll be the death of me yet. How do you expect to handle the sausages for tonight's fry-up with hands like a dust pan? Do you want to give everyone food poisoning?'

'We've all brought along forks,' said Nobby. 'We

won't have to touch our sausages with our hands. We can eat them by remote control, if you see what I mean.'

'That's no excuse, you little germ-spreader,' said Akela. He walked into the centre of the hall to address all his Cubs. 'Listen, lads! One of the first things you learn when you join the Cub Scouts is how to keep your hands, nails and teeth clean. That's not just because it's the normal, healthy, decent thing to do, or because I want you all to look like little tailors' dummies. There is a practical reason for it. When we go camping, you will be expected to take your turn at preparing food, and if your hands aren't clean, you may spread all sorts of germs, which could make some of you ill. Now I want each of you in turn to go to the washroom to wash your hands and brush your nails, and when you come back, we can have our Friday night fry-up.'

The Cubs cheered and filed to the washroom to clean themselves up. Akela got out the Pack portable gas stove, placed it in the centre of the hall on a biscuit tin lid, and lit it. When the Cubs returned, they got out their sausages and put them in the frying-pan, under Akela's supervision. The smell of the sizzling sausages made their insides knot-up in agony. The taste of hot-dogs was one of their greatest pleasures. Nobby wolfed down his second and last sausage.

'Goo!' he said, 'they were good. It's worth going through all the misery of having a good scrub for such a meal.'

Snowy nodded. 'It sure is, Nobby. Anyway, I want to go down to my Dad's chemist shop tomorrow to get a new nail brush. Want to come along?'

Nobby nodded. 'I need a nail brush and a nail file, Snowy,' he said. 'If I can get my mum to let me have next month's pocket money in advance, I might just be able to afford one or the other. I did have a nail file once, but it broke when I used it as an ink-pellet catapult. I tried using Dad's rasp on my nails, but I gave that up as a bad job. I nearly filed off my fingers. It didn't half hurt.'

'We'll see what Dad has in his shop tomorrow, eh?'

Akela interrupted their conversation by calling for

their attention so he could give them a demonstration on how to make a can of tea.

'Can't we have lemonade?' asked Nobby.

'You need something hot tonight,' said Akela.

'Can't we have hot lemonade?'

'If you don't like tea, you needn't have it,' said Akela curtly.

Nobby, however, changed his mind when he saw the hot, strong tea ladled out, to go with the bread and honey.

'I think I'll try a little,' he said, holding out his tin cup. 'Just one and a half cup-fulls, please.'

'What, all at once?' said Akela.

Akela gave him what was left in the can. That, laced with plenty of sugar, went down well after the sausages, with the bread and honey.

'I like tea,' burped Nobby. 'It's not bad when it's made properly.'

'Then you'll have to learn how to make it,' said Akela. Akela blew his whistle. 'Listen, lads, I want to show you how to turn off the gas-stove, and wash and tidy up the dirty crockery and cutlery, so as not to spread germs.'

Akela got his Cubs to tidy up the place. The open windows soon cleared the air, so that by the time the flag was lowered, no one could have guessed there had been a recent fry-up in the hall. Each Cub, however, had a warm and comfortable feeling in his stomach.

'See you tomorrow lads, for the fête,' said Akela, 'with clean hands, nails and teeth.'

On Saturday morning, Snowy and Nobby went along to the high street chemist's shop to see Snowy's father about some nail brushes.

'Yes, I've got some nail sets,' said Mr White. He broke off to serve a customer. The Cubs waited until he was free to come back to them. 'I want you to do a job first. The boxes of camera equipment have arrived. They're in the back passage. I want you to take them upstairs to the empty room, mark the contents on the sides with a felt-tip pen, and stack them neatly against the wall so I can get just what I want quickly. Understand?'

'Have you got a box of nail brushes?' asked Nobby.

Snowy pulled him away by the arm. 'Come on, Nobby.'

The Cubs went upstairs to mark and stack the boxes against the wall. In that empty room, they felt miles away from the world, until they heard a scraping noise on the window sill. Snowy looked around and got the shock of his life when he saw a man at the window, but he need not have been alarmed. The man was a house painter and decorator.

Nobby pressed his little button nose on the window-pane to look at the intruder, but he recoiled in horror when the painter dabbed his brush at Nobby's nose.

'Gerroff!' bawled Nobby. 'I don't want my nose painting.'

The painter smiled and wiped the paint stain off the glass with a rag. Snowy, very conscious this week, of his hands, noticed that the house painter had fingers as fine and delicate as a pianist, as he opened the window.

'Do you want some gum, boys?' said the painter in a Cockney accent. He felt in his pockets.

'Oh, yes,' said Nobby. 'I like gum.'

The painter fished a pad of sticky labels out of his pocket, tore one off and gave it to Nobby.

''ere, lick the gum off that,' he laughed.

Nobby looked dejected. He licked the back of the gummed label and stuck it on top of the painter's ladder.

''ere, Puddin' Face,' said the painter, 'since you are such a good sport, you can have a real sweet.' The painter again fished in his pockets and brought out a roll of mint sweets. ''ere, go ahead,' he said. 'They ain't poison. If they are, bring 'em back and I'll change 'em for you.'

Nobby took a sweet. 'Oh, thanks,' he said when he saw it was genuine.

''ere, you help yourself too, sonny,' he said to Snowy.

'Oh, thanks,' said Snowy, taking a sweet. 'Thanks very much.'

'What are you doing all dressed up in uniform, holding a jamboree or something?'

'No, the Scouts are having a spring fête to raise money for a boat. We promised to go and give them a hand as soon as we've finished this job.'

'Boat, eh? Cor, you lads do have a nice time of it, don't you? I nearly joined the Cubs once, but I didn't. At that time I thought they were a bunch of cissies, always washing and brushing-up.'

Snowy reddened. 'What's wrong with that? Guardsmen wash and brush-up more than anyone. Have you seen the Trooping of the Colour, when the guardsmen parade before the Queen? They aren't cissies. Besides, Cub Scouting isn't all washing and brushing-up.'

'You're quite right there, little fella. I never joined the Cubs, but I wish I 'ad. I would have met a lot better set of lads than those I did mix with. Bad lot, they were. Cor, some of 'em I met would take the laces out of your boots, if you gave 'em 'alf a chance. You couldn't trust 'em an inch. I regret not 'aving joined the Cub Scouts, but you can't turn the clock back, can you?'

'You can join the Chelsea pensioners,' suggested Nobby.

The painter laughed. 'I might do that, when I'm

ninety. Imagine that lot of old codgers sittin' round a
camp fire singin', *We're ridin' along on a crest of a
wave*. Hey, you're stoppin' a workin' man gettin' on
with his job. Now you don't want me to get the sack
from your ole man, do you?'

'No, don't mind us,' said Snowy.

''ave a good time at your spring fête, eh? I 'ope you
get your boat.'

'Oh, thanks, thanks very much,' said Snowy.

The painter lowered the window and got on with
his job. The Cubs got on with theirs. The boxes,
marked, 'Cameras – Still and Ciné', 'Exposure
Meters', 'Projectors', were stacked neatly against the
wall. The Cubs went downstairs to see if there was
anything else Mr White would like doing.

'No, that's all I want today,' said Mr White.

Again he was interrupted, this time by the painter.

'Is it all right if I leave my ladder in the back
passage as usual, Mr White?'

'Sure!' said Mr White. 'How's the job going?'

'Fine, I'll 'ave it finished on Monday, if the weather 'olds.'

The painter slid his ladder into the back passage, slipped his jacket over his overalls and left the premises. Mr White finished serving another customer.

'That Harry Bates, he's a marvel,' said Mr White, nodding after the painter. 'He's making a real good job of my shop front. He takes twice as long to do it but only charges half as much as other painters and decorators I know. Quite frankly, I don't know how he does it.'

When Mr White was free, he gave each of the boys a nail set and a toothbrush, in return for the work they had done for him.

'Goo, thanks, Mr White,' said Nobby, 'Anytime you want your shop sweeping out, just let me know.'

'I'll do that,' said Mr White, turning to serve another customer.

But Snowy was not at all happy. He waited until his father was free.

'Are . . . are you sure that house painter is trustworthy, Dad?' he said.

'What do you mean?' said Mr White.

'It's . . . it's just that he seems a bit suspicious to me. He watched us as we stacked away the camera equipment when he was upstairs, painting the window.

And I noticed he had very fine fingers, like a pick-pocket, not at all like a painter and decorator. And you said yourself that you didn't know how he could afford to paint the shop at the rate he charges. Burglars have been known to disguise themselves as painters or window-cleaners, so they can look over a place . . .'

'I don't believe it!' snapped Mr White. 'Just you be sure of your facts before you make accusations like that. Harry Bates is a very reliable young man as far as I'm concerned, and I know how important it is to keep costs down, especially when you're trying to start up a new business.'

'But . . . but what if he is a . . .'

'Oh, no, really,' said Mr White, turning to serve a new customer.

Snowy knew this was neither the time nor the place to talk to his father.

'It's a good nail-file,' said Nobby, 'but it doesn't half hurt when you stick it right under your nails.'

'Let's go upstairs to the bathroom,' said Snowy, feeling out of tune with the world. 'You can try out your nail-brush there.'

'Can I?' said Nobby. 'Oh, thanks.'

Nobby fell up the stairs to the bathroom. There, he went through the elaborate procedures of brushing his nails. He even used the nail-brush to part his hair, and brush down his trousers, and because his shoes were a bit dusty, he gave them a little brush too. Snowy just watched him vacantly. He was still uneasy.

'You know, Nobby, I'm still a bit suspicious about that painter. I think he could be a burglar. Now that he knows where the camera equipment is stored, he could break in through the skylight tonight and steal the lot.'

'Steal it?' said Nobby. 'How do you know? What are you going to do?'

'I don't know, I don't know. I've just got this feeling, that's all. I've mentioned it to Dad, but he doesn't seem very interested at the moment. I . . . I don't know what to do, really.'

'I know,' said Nobby, excitedly. 'We can dial nine-nine-nine and get the police to come here at midnight, and when the burglar comes through the skylight, they can grab him and take him off to prison.'

'Ah, the police will want definite evidence before they dare waste their time . . . Whatever we do, we must do ourselves.'

'I'm . . . I'm not coming down here at midnight to catch a burglar,' said Nobby. 'It . . . it will be dark. My mum wouldn't let me come anyway.'

'I don't mean that. We . . . we'll have to think of something else.'

'Oh,' said Nobby, very much relieved. 'I know.' He

beamed at himself in the mirror. 'We can hang a mirror on the wall, and when the burglar looks in, he'll frighten himself to death . . .'

Snowy looked the other way.

'I know.' Nobby waved the nail-brush in front of Snowy's face. 'I've got a toy police car with a siren and flashing lights. If we wind it up, and put it behind a box, when the box is moved, the car will come out, wailing and flashing, and the burglar will get the shock of his life . . .'

Snowy snorted.

'We could tie a brick on the end of a rope,' went on Nobby, 'and dangle it overhead with the other end under a box. When the burglar moves the box, the brick will drop on his head.' Nobby was full of ideas. 'We could fix up a camera, so that when the burglar trips over a wire, the camera takes his picture which we can give to the police to identify him.'

But Snowy was not impressed. 'And what if Dad wants to get a camera out for a customer? Do you think he'd like to stand on a toy car, trip over a wire and get a picture of himself looking in the mirror to see himself hit on the head with a brick?'

Nobby shrugged his shoulders.

'Oh, we've just got to hope the stuff won't be stolen,' said Snowy, 'but we can still make it difficult for any burglar. If I can find some rope in the back, we can tie the boxes together, and Dad will still be able to get the cameras out one at a time. I think there's some cord in the back.'

Snowy did find plenty of tough nylon cord amongst a few empty crates in the back, and he went upstairs to secure the boxes as best he could. Nobby helped him, using variations of every knot he had seen in the Cubs, and some knots which nobody in the world had seen. Snowy knew that anyone with a sharp knife could cut through the cord, but it would take time, and it would be inconvenient, and Snowy did not want to make it convenient for any would be burglar. Then he got the shock of his life. He glanced at the window and saw the burglar watching him.

The man opened the window. 'You are makin' a real good job of that, whatever it is. What are you doing?'

'Blah, blah, bah!' Nobby blabbered. 'We . . . we were only tying up these boxes so when you come here at midnight to burgle the shop, you can't get them.'

Snowy reddened with embarrassment. Nobby was too outspoken. He had practically accused the painter of being a burglar, on no more evidence than a hunch of Snowy's. The painter opened the window a little wider.

'Yeowh!' yelled Nobby, dashing away to hide behind the stack of boxes.

'We were tying up these boxes to make it difficult for any burglar to take them,' said Snowy.

'That's a very good idea,' said the painter, 'a very good idea indeed. I wish everyone would take as much care with their property. If they did, my young brother might not be in prison today. You know what 'e did? He was passin' one of these open-topped sports cars parked in the street, and he saw a camera lying on the seat. Now my brother was a bit short of cash, you see, we come from a very poor family, so 'e picked up this 'ere camera. Next thing he knew, 'e was caught by the police and sentenced to six months. But if you ask me, the man who should be in prison is the motorist who tempted my brother. He doesn't deserve to 'ave property if 'e can't look after it.'

Snowy shrugged his shoulders, and put the last few knots in the cord.

'Mind you,' went on the painter, 'don't think that I would ever dream of burglin' your place. Not me. I've got my own little business to keep me. It doesn't pay much, but I get by. One of these days though, I'll be the best known painter in the country.'

'I wish you every success,' said Snowy. He looked around at the boxes which were positively secured in a mesh of cord. 'We must be going now. The spring fête starts at two. We've got to set up our equipment before we open.'

'Enjoy yourselves then. 'ope you get your boat soon.'

'Thanks.'

Snowy and Nobby slid out of the room and closed the door behind them.

'Do you think he'll still steal the equipment?' said Nobby.

'We've done what we can,' said Snowy.

As it turned out, the equipment was not stolen, nor was the shop broken into. Harry Bates finished his job, much to Mr White's satisfaction, collected his money, though he did forget to take his paraffin burner, and left. Anyway, he left on the friendliest of terms, so it seemed that Snowy's hunch had been wide off the mark.

Some time later, however, when Mr White discovered the paraffin burner, he asked Snowy and Nobby to return it to nineteen Jackson Street, the address shown on the receipted bill. Snowy and Nobby had not been to that part of Billington before. They found half of the houses in the street had been pulled down, and the other half looked as though they were about to be pulled down. The house in question, number nineteen, had one of its upstairs windows boarded up with hardboard. A woman in curlers, pinafore and slippers stood at the open door.

'Excuse me, does Mr Bates live here, Mr Harry Bates?' Snowy asked.

'Mr Bates, huh!' said the woman. 'He's upstairs and he hasn't paid his rent for three weeks! She snorted at the Cubs and shuffled back to a back room.

Snowy and Nobby tip-toed onto the bare boards of the passageway. The interior of the house was in the same state of decay as the outside. Plaster was hanging from the walls. The woodwork sadly needed a coat of paint.

A man hurried down the narrow stairs. It was Harry Bates. He had a folder under his arm. Snowy held out the paraffin burner to him.

'Your burner, Mr Bates,' said Snowy.

Harry Bates brushed them aside. 'Keep it,' he growled. He stopped at the front door and turned around. ''ere, are you the two Cubs from the chemist's in the high street?' He smiled as he recognised them. ''ere, I 'ave to thank you for savin' my life.'

'Saving your life?' echoed Nobby. He looked at Snowy. 'We didn't save his life, did we?'

Harry Bates laughed. 'You most certainly did, in a way. I don't suppose you know that I was plannin' to burgle the chemist's shop. I'm an artist who couldn't sell 'is paintings. Last Saturday in sheer desperation, I planned to burgle the shop, but you two scared me off. I came back 'ere, and as I knew it would not be so easy to get away with a burglary, I 'ad another go at showin' my drawings to a publisher. You know what? A publisher in Manchester liked them. He asked me to illustrate a complete book of nursery rhymes. It's a year's work for me. Look . . .'

The artist opened his folder to show the Cubs some of his drawings. Snowy gasped. They were very good. The objects seemed to stand out of the page.

'They are very good!' was all Snowy could say.

'How do you get some things to seem so near and some to be so far away?' asked Nobby.

'Perspective and tonal depth,' said the artist.

'Eh?' said Nobby.

The artist showed his drawings in which Jack was falling down a really steep hill, Little Miss Muffet was really frightened by a spider, Mary's lamb really had fleece as white as snow, Humpty Dumpty was really a smashed up egg, and the cow really jumped over the moon.

'They are very, very good,' said Snowy, still filled with wonder.

'The problem is I have to do two colour pictures for the front and back covers, and I want to get them just right. A good front cover sells more books than the words inside . . .' Suddenly the artist beamed at Snowy. ''ere, you would make the perfect Little Boy Blue! Perfect! I can just imagine a front cover picture in full colour of you dressed in blue, blowing a horn. Great! Perfect! Just what I've been lookin' for. Listen, get you parents' permission, your Cubmaster's and anybody else interested. You will be known all over the country in a couple of years time . . .'

Little Nobby Clark pushed in front of Snowy.

'Can I be Little Boy Blue too?'

'There's only one Little Boy Blue.'

'Oh!' Nobby was downcast, but he soon brightened. 'Can I be Little Jack Horner eating a pork pie?'

'I've done Little Jack Horner.'

'Oh. How about old King Cole playing a fiddle?'

'You're too skinny!'

'Jack and the beanstalk fighting the giant. I'd be good as Jack and the beanstalk.'

'Beanstalk maybe, but not Jack. Besides, that's a story, not a nursery rhyme. What can I do with you? Ah, there's nobody with a pie-face like yours in nursery rhymes.'

Nobby was downcast. The artist turned back to Snowy.

'These books, I'm told, will be sold to primary schools all over the English-speakin' world. You'll . . . you'll be world famous . . .' Suddenly the artist broke off and looked back at Nobby. He snapped his fingers. 'I know who you can be. Little Boy Blue can be on the back cover, you can be on the front. Your face will fit perfectly – perfectly! I can see your face on the front cover now, with your shaggy hair, squashed-up nose, big grin, green goggly eyes, sticky-out ears, puddin' face, pie-crust brow. You'll be world famous. The kids will love you.'

'Who will I be?' asked Nobby. 'Who, who, who?'

'Georgie Porgie!' said the artist.

5 · The desk of the Earl of Houston

As for the spring fête, it was organised by the Scouts who were hoping to raise money to buy an old barge, which they planned to convert into a canal cruiser. The hall was crowded with visitors, flocking round the tables to buy bargains, goods which had been donated to the Troop. These bargains included pots of jam and cakes made by the mothers of the Troop, groceries, old books and games, plants and vegetables. Outside, on the lawn, other Cubs and Scouts had set up their stalls to challenge the skill of the customers.

Snowy's and Nobby's contribution to this was a little film show, held in the Headquarters' cloakroom, which had been prepared for the occasion. Snowy had borrowed his father's ciné projector and half a dozen old classic films. The projector, he had set on a stand, just inside the doorway, to face the screen on the opposite wall. The window had been blacked out, and six folding chairs, all that could be comfortably housed, had been set up for the audience.

'Roll up, roll up,' called Snowy, standing outside

the cloakroom. 'The film show is about to begin. Take your seats for the film show. Tickets only five pence each.'

'Come and see King Kong,' said Nobby. 'King Kong's a giant gorilla. Come and see him knock down sky-scrapers, eat people and fight aeroplanes. It's a lovely film. Come and see King Kong. Frighten yourself to death for only five pence.'

At that moment, a stoutish old woman happened to be passing by, carrying a basket loaded with vegetables.

'Ah, Mrs Cooper,' said Akela, spotting her. 'I haven't seen you for ages. How are you?'

'My bloomin' feet aren't half killing me,' said the woman, putting down her basket.

'You can sit down in here for five pence,' said Nobby, 'and you can watch King Kong at the same time.'

'Don't interrupt,' corrected Akela, sternly. He looked at the woman's loaded basket. 'I see you've been supporting our Scouts' fête.'

'Aye, I've been doing me shoppin'. Your stuff's a lot cheaper than what they sell at the shops. Don't know where they get the prices from, that I don't.'

Akela nodded. 'And how's your Charlie getting on?'

The old woman beamed. 'Ah, Charlie, he's fine. It doesn't seem long since you two were Boy Scouts together, in the old hut they had before you built this new hall. Charlie's in Canada now, you know, but he expects to be home before Christmas. I only heard from him last week, it was.' Mrs Cooper looked about her. 'My feet are killing me!'

Nobby put up his hand. 'Please, miss, you can sit down in here, and watch King Kong. Only five pence.'

'Only two and a half pence for senior citizens,' said Snowy.

'Why don't you go in for a few minutes,' said Akela, taking Mrs Cooper by the arm. 'Watch the show on me.' Akela winked at Snowy. 'Don't charge for this one, Snowy. I'll square up with you later.'

Snowy nodded and held open the door.

'Come in, Mrs Cooper. You can take a seat any-where.'

Mrs Cooper came into the cloakroom-cum-cinema and sat in one of the six fabric covered tubular steel chairs. She pushed off her shoes.

'Ooh!' she groaned in relief. 'That's better!'

Nobby came up to her with a tray on which were half-a-dozen chocolate ices.

'Do you want a choc-ice, missus?' said Nobby.

'No, I don't,' said Mrs Cooper.

'Don't worry, don't worry,' said Nobby, I'll be round again in the interval. If you want a choc-ice before that, give me a shout, eh?'

With that, he tried to squeeze in front of Mrs Cooper to reach the other side of the tiny room.

'Excuse me,' he said.

He trod on her stockinged foot. She let out a yell and gave him a push to ward him off. Nobby fell flat on his face, his tray clattered to the floor, and his ice-creams shot off in all directions.

'Oh, sorry,' he said, as he scrambled to his knees. He pushed the folding chairs out of his way, and re-trieved his ice-creams. 'Don't worry, I've got them all,' he said.

He gathered up all the ice-creams replaced them on the tray and propped the tray on a nearby empty chair. He clattered past two other folding chairs and stood in front of the silver screen. For a moment he forgot what he wanted to say, then he remembered.

'We've got to wait until all the seats are full before we start the show,' he announced, 'so until then, I'll tell you about the film. It's about a great big gorilla called King Kong . . .'

'And you're his little brother, Thin Kong, I suppose,' said Mrs Cooper. 'Why don't you shut up? I came in here for five minutes peace, and all you do is gabble, gabble, bang, clatter, clatter.'

Akela slipped into the room and nodded at Snowy.

'Start the show now,' he advised. 'If anyone comes in later, we can let them stay longer to see a second run through.'

Snowy nodded. He, like Akela, was anxious to keep the peace. He operated his projector switch.

'Lights, please, Nobby.'

'Lights, yes, lights,' said Nobby. 'I'll switch out the lights.'

He squeezed past the row of chairs to go to the light switch just as Akela switched out the lights. Nobby, suddenly finding himself in the dark, tripped over the mains lead to the projector. Snowy grabbed the projector to prevent it being pulled onto the floor, with the result that the plug was pulled out of the mains socket and the projector stopped running.

Akela switched on the lights again. 'What are you doing on the floor?'

'Oh, I've pulled the lead out,' grunted Nobby. 'I'll put it back.'

Nobby crawled under a chair to put in the plug.

Mrs Cooper turned round to see what the commotion was all about. When Nobby put in the plug, the projector started running again, whirring away.

'Hey,' said Mrs Cooper, before the lights went out again. 'Is that one of those projector things that shows films? Does it show films you can take yourself?'

'Yes, it takes eight millimetre films, that's what most home movie makers use.'

'And would it show a film Charlie sent from Canada?'

'I should think so,' said Akela. 'Film sizes are standard throughout the world. This projector takes standard eight and super eight millimetre films. I shouldn't think yours is any different from that.'

'If I get it, could you show it here?' said Mrs Cooper. 'I haven't seen it myself yet.'

'Yes, why not? No problem. Where is it?'

'It's at home in the old mahogany desk.'

Akela laughed. 'You've still got that old desk? Must be worth something now. Real Victorian masterpiece, that is, made to last.'

'Bah! It's a waste of good space,' said Mrs Cooper.

'Waste of good space?' said Akela. 'I remember you

used to say it was your pride and joy, and you'd rather starve than get rid of it.'

'Maybe I did once, but . . . it's too big for me to keep clean and dusted now. Anyway, that's where Charlie's film is.'

'Why not send Nobby to pick up your film, Mrs Cooper?' said Akela. 'He's a bit clumsy, but he's honest.'

'Would he?'

'Sure! You'd better go with him, Snowy, in case he goes in the wrong house. I'll look after the projector. You know where Mount Avenue is, up by the railway station?'

'Number eight,' said Mrs Cooper. 'Here's the key. You can go straight in. In the front room, there's a great big mahogany desk. You can't miss it. There's a film in the bottom drawer of the headboard, nearest the door, in a yellow box.'

'All right,' said Snowy. 'We'll find it.'

'You might as well take the shopping basket,' said Akela.

'Oh, this is nice of you,' said Mrs Cooper, taking her purse from the basket. 'You can leave the basket on the desk. I'll unpack it myself when I get home.'

Snowy and Nobby picked up the shopping basket between them.

'We'll be back in ten minutes,' said Snowy.

'And don't forget to lock up before you come back,' said Akela.

'All right,' said Snowy.

Snowy and Nobby had little difficulty in finding eight Mount Avenue. It was a tiny terraced cottage, which had seen better days. Snowy opened the door with the latch key, and went inside. Nobby crept behind him like a burglar. Snowy went through a half open door into the cosy front room.

'Anyone in?' called Nobby nervously.

The front room was small, yet just inside the door was the biggest desk Snowy had ever seen. It was of elaborately carved mahogany, built like a battleship. It had two tiers, one on top of the other. The lower tier was as large as the average dining table, with three

deep drawers on either side. In the opening between the drawers, was a matching revolving chair. The top tier was a carved headboard, which stretched up to the ceiling. There was even a thick plate glass mirror in the centre of the headboard, flanked by two towers of little bureau drawers.

'You could play ping-pong on the desk top, and you could hide in here,' said Nobby, opening a large drawer and putting his head inside.

'Don't be nosey,' said Snowy, putting the basket on top.

'Mrs Cooper said the film is in the headboard bottom drawer.'

Snowy looked in the bottom little drawer. It was full of letters, bills, papers, and buttons, but he also saw the little yellow box. It was eight millimetre film, which would fit the projector.

'Got it!' said Snowy. 'Let's get back, Nobby. They'll be waiting for us.'

It didn't take long before they locked up and returned to the fête. By this time, the cloakroom cinema was full, and a show was in progress, but they did not have long to wait before the first film was over. It was a Laurel and Hardy film. Akela took Mrs Cooper's film from Snowy.

'I hope the rest of the audience won't mind us showing an extra film in this performance,' said Akela, as he rewound the previous film. 'This lady, Mrs Cooper, has a film which was sent to her by her son in Canada.'

'I haven't seen it myself,' said Mrs Cooper.

Akela fitted and projected the film. It showed, in the white forested wastes of Northern Canada, bulldozers and lorries clearing a way to build towering electricity pylons. The men were dressed in furs, like Eskimos, to keep out the cold. Their breaths, as they exhaled, were immediately vapourised in the cold air, but they were a happy lot. They grinned as they ladled out steaming mugs of tea. One of the men, a slim youth of about Akela's age, waved at the camera.

'That's Charlie!' said Mrs Cooper. 'I can't hear him.'

'This isn't a sound movie,' said Akela.

'It's a bleak place to work,' said someone in the audience. 'He must be making plenty of money in that job.'

'Charlie went to Canada to make his fortune,' said Mrs Cooper. 'He'll be coming home at Christmas.'

Finally Charlie pointed to a message he had chalked on the side of his hut. It said: 'See you at Christmas, Mum.'

'I'd better get rid of that old desk quickly, to make room for Charlie when he comes home,' said Mrs Cooper as the lights came on.

Akela smiled. 'You'll miss that old desk, Mrs Cooper. I remember the chemistry experiments Charlie and I used to do on it when we were Cubs. It's a wonder we didn't set the thing on fire.'

'You made some stains on it with all your chemicals, said Mrs Cooper, 'but you never did any real harm. If Charlie wants a desk when he comes home, he can buy himself a nice new one. A second-hand dealer has already offered me four pounds fifty for it . . .'

'Four pounds fifty!' shrieked Akela in surprise. 'It's . . . it's worth ten times that.'

'That may be, but four pounds fifty is the best offer I've had.'

'Why not take it to the auction rooms in the high street? You'll get more than four pounds fifty for it there.'

'Aye, an' it'll cost me two pounds to have a lorry to take it there,' said Mrs Cooper. 'I haven't got two pounds.'

'I'll tell you what I'll do. After the fête, I'll ask the Scouts to take it down to the auction rooms for you. They've borrowed a handcart for the day. The auction rooms are open until ten o'clock tonight, and there's always a good crowd there on Saturdays. You'll be able to get a quick sale at a fair price. How does that suit you?'

'That's fine, that's fine, that's fine. I'll be pleased to

get rid of that old thing. It's been taking up too much room for too long now.'

'All right, Mrs Cooper, we'll be along after we've tidied up here. Snowy, carry on with the film show, will you?'

Snowy took his place behind the projector as Akela left the room with Mrs Cooper.

Snowy had just finished checking his cash takings when Akela returned.

'How did the film show go, Snowy?'

'We've made one pound ninety,' said Snowy, 'but I've got five pence more than the tickets I've sold.'

'Oh, I'm sorry, I forgot to tell you. I put five pence in for Mrs Cooper and didn't take a ticket.'

'Then we're all square. One pound ninety, that should help the Scouts a bit with their barge.'

'Good!' Akela looked round at Nobby who was making shadows on the silver screen. 'Hey, clever Dick, how much did you make out of the ice-creams, or did you whoof the lot yourself?'

Nobby frowned. 'Oh!' he said. He fished a used tobacco tin out of his pocket and opened it up to reveal his takings.

'Clegg's let me have twenty choc-ices at three pence each, and I sold them at the selling price of five pence each. Twenty times five is . . . Nobby went through his table and counted on his fingers. 'That's hundred pence – that's a pound.' He counted out the money. That's a pound.'

'And where did you get the sixty pence to buy the choc-ices in the first place?' asked Akela, suspiciously.

'Oh, I cleaned out the inside of Mr Clegg's van for that,' said Nobby, giving Akela the money.

Akela took the money out of Nobby's little grubby hands. The words seemed to stick in his throat.

'Have you . . . have you got that great feeling Cub Scouts have when they have done a good turn for somebody?' he asked.

Nobby shrugged his shoulders.

'Well, you should have,' went on Akela. 'I'm . . . I'm proud of you, Nobby. This money . . . will help the Scouts with their barge, and . . . when it's ready for cruising, and it's our turn to borrow it . . . you can be the first to take the wheel. That I promise you.'

'Really?' said Nobby, somewhat overwhelmed. 'Oh, thanks.'

Akela pulled himself together. 'Well, I'm off now to help the Scouts with Mrs Cooper's desk. Mrs Cooper is a poor widow now, but she's got a heart of gold. I can't remember how many times I had my tea at her place. She hasn't had much fun in life, and I like to help her a bit when I can.'

'When you help somebody,' goggled Nobby, 'do you

get that great feeling a Cub Scout has when he's done somebody a good turn?'

Akela laughed. 'Well . . . yes . . . I do, sometimes. Anyway, this desk of Mrs Cooper's, it's a bit heavy, so I doubt if you two can help any . . .'

'We could carry the drawers,' suggested Snowy.

Oh, all right. After you've tided up this place, I'll meet you outside.'

Half a dozen of the burliest Scouts pushed and heaved the borrowed handcart out of the gateway. After locking up the hall, Akela, with Snowy and Nobby, followed them to Mount Avenue.

It only took a minute for the Scouts to lift the head-board off the lower section of the desk, and put it on the handcart. Then with whoops and shouts, they

wheeled their cargo away down Mount Avenue to the auction rooms in the high street.

Akela closed the door behind them. He scratched his head.

'Apart from taking out the drawers, I don't see what you can do until the Scouts return with the hand cart,' he said to Snowy and Nobby.

Snowy nodded. He took out a drawer.

'Would you like a cup of tea?' asked Mrs Cooper.

'That's very kind of you,' said Akela, going to join her in the back kitchen. 'Can I give you a hand?'

As Snowy took out the remainder of the drawers, Nobby slipped out of his shoes and climbed on top of the partially dismantled desk.

'And now entering the ring is Joe (Man) Mountain,' Nobby announced, then he began wrestling with himself on the broad desk top.

Snowy stacked the drawers out of the way for the time being, under the front room table. He then noticed that the drawers from either side of the desk were of different lengths. Snowy frowned. He could think of no reason why matching drawers should be as different as this – almost a hundred millimetres.

Nobby fell on the floor.

' . . . and Man Mountain has been thrown out of the ring,' he announced, 'but not for long – he's back on his feet and in the ring again.'

Nobby leapt back onto the desk top.

As Snowy could still think of no reason why matching drawers should be of different lengths, he looked under the desk to see if the housings were different. They were. There was less space for the drawers on the right hand side than on the left. The back panel on the right hand side was farther forward than the panel on the other side – but why? The desk was the same width on both sides.

Snowy looked around a bit more.

The rear legs of the desk were carved with a twisted arrangement of vines. On the right hand leg, the vines appeared to be broken in two places, as if a fifty millimetre slice had been cut out and re-inserted, not quite accurately.

Snowy got hold of the segment and gave it a twist. The segment turned until the vine pattern was properly lined up. But if that segment could be turned one way, surely it could be turned the other way.

Snowy turned it the other way. There was a loud click, and a panel in the side of the desk opened a centimetre. Snowy took hold of the panel, and eased it open, he found it was the front of a tall, narrow drawer. The drawer was crammed with drawings and papers.

'Submit, submit, submit,' croaked Nobby, lying

over the edge of the desk with his arm around his throat.

I've found a concealed drawer,' shouted Snowy to the kitchen.

Akela charged through the kitchen doorway.

'Get off there, you little monkey,' he bawled at Nobby. He slid off the desk top. 'If I catch you on there again, I'll take you to the auction rooms and sell you . . .'

'He's not doing any harm,' said Mrs Cooper, coming into the front room. 'I can remember you and Charlie doing just the same when you were his age.'

Akela reddened. 'Well, that was different . . .'

'Different, my foot! What have you got there, boy?' the woman said to Snowy.

'I . . . I found this drawer in the side of the desk,' said Snowy. 'It's . . . it's still full of papers.'

'I didn't know it was part of the desk,' said Mrs Cooper.

Akela looked into the drawer. 'Then you didn't know about these papers?

'No, my word, I didn't!'

They took the papers from the drawer and spread them on the wide desk top. There was a mass of drawings and letters. The drawings were of pieces of machinery. One of them showed what looked like a squashed up electric motor.

'They must be Charlie's,' said Mrs Cooper. 'He was always drawing and designing things. And here are some letters.' She gave a pile of letters to Akela. 'Can you read them? I haven't got me glasses.'

Akela looked at a letter.

'Dear Mr Cooper,' he read out. 'Regret I cannot grant you a bank loan unless you are able to offer some form of security.'

Akela looked at another letter. 'Regret we cannot finance development work on your invention unless you let us have full details of your designs.' He picked out another letter. 'Regret we cannot offer you the thousand pounds you require unless you can give us an adequate demonstration.'

Mrs Cooper sniffed. 'Oh dear, you don't think Charlie got himself in debt, do you?'

'Oh, no,' said Akela. 'Machines need money for development, that's what banks are for, if you've got security.'

Akela had another look at the engineering drawings.

'Looks like a new type of electric motor,' he said. 'Oh, isn't it compact? It's only a tenth of the size of conventional electric motors of the same power rating.' Akela stared into space. 'So that's why Charlie wanted the money so badly – to develop his motor.'

'He'll have the money when he comes back from Canada,' said Mrs Cooper.

'He will, he will, if I know Charlie,' said Akela, 'and if this motor works . . . Everybody uses electric motors in refrigerators, vacuum cleaners, lawn-mowers, electric drills . . . If Charlie's invention works, and he can produce a better, cheaper motor than any-one else, why, he could grab the world markets!'

Akela folded up the papers.

'Look after these drawings, Mrs Cooper, until Charlie is ready to collect them. At Christmas, we'll have a new British inventor in our midst.'

'You don't think Charlie will be angry with me for getting rid of the desk, do you?'

'No, no, Mrs Cooper. Charlie won't ever be angry with you. What he wants are his designs. Keep them safely for him, lock them away and don't let anyone see them. These drawings may one day bring in hundreds of thousands of pounds.'

'Really?' said Mrs Cooper. 'And Charlie did them?'

'Yes, Mrs Cooper.'

'Ooh, he is a dark horse, just like his father.'

Snowy had another look inside the concealed com-partment to make sure he had not overlooked anything. Just then, the Scouts returned with the handcart. With them was a gentleman.

'I'm Mr Braithwaite,' the gentleman introduced

himself, nervously. 'I am an antique dealer. I saw your headboard in the auction rooms. If the rest of it is in a sound condition, perhaps I can make you an offer, or sell it on your behalf.'

'An offer?' said Mrs Cooper. How much?'

The antique dealer examined the piece.

'It's got a concealed drawer,' said Snowy, showing him how it worked.

'Magnificent, magnificent,' said the antique dealer. 'Unless I am mistaken, this is part of a suite. The matching chairs, bookcase and table are owned by the ninth Earl of Houston.'

'Earl of Houston!' said Mrs Cooper. 'My grandfather used to work for the old earl years ago. He gave my grandfather this desk on his retirement.'

'So I am right,' said the antique dealer. 'This will fetch a pretty penny at Christie's, if I am not mistaken.'

'How much?' asked Mrs Cooper.

'Far more than I'm able to pay for it,' said the antique dealer reluctantly, 'but if you let me sell it for you, I'll get the best price I can, and charge ten per cent for my services.'

'How much . . .?'

'Oh, the desk and chair together would bring about two thousand five hundred pounds, I'd say, less my two hundred and fifty, that leaves about two thousand, two hundred and fifty.'

'Two thousand two hundred and fifty?' gasped Mrs Cooper, hardly able to believe her ears. She looked at Akela.

'Seems all right to me,' said Akela. 'Ten per cent is the standard rate for dealers, but I'll make enquiries for you, Mrs Cooper, to see if I can get a better rate.'

'Better than two thousand two hundred and fifty?' said Mrs Cooper. 'Oh, I'll be able to give Charlie a nice Christmas when he comes home. Oh, dear, let's all have a cup of tea.'

Snowy watched Mrs Cooper dash off to the kitchen. It was obvious that today had been one of her happiest for many years.

Suddenly Snowy had that great feeling a Cub Scout has when he has helped, even in some small way, to do a good turn for someone else.

6 · Medal of bronze

Snowy rode his bicycle confidently along the main
road. He wore his Cub Scout uniform, and whenever
he wore his uniform, he sensed people were watching
him. On this morning however, he knew he was being
watched every bit of the way. On this morning, Akela
had arranged a cycle test and some of the older Scouts
had volunteered to act as marshals along the route to
ensure that none of the Cubs got into difficulty.

At the corner, among the shoppers, outside a little
antique shop, he saw Akela with a notepad and pencil
in his hand.

'Good lad, Snowy,' said Akela, making a tick on his
pad. 'Stop just around the corner.'

Snowy gave the correct signal for a left turn,
turned the corner and stopped his cycle at the kerb.
Behind him came Nobby. Nobby jammed on his
brakes and skidded to a halt so that his front tyre
stopped not more than a millimetre from Snowy's rear
reflector. Nobby turned his head to look back at
Akela.

'Have I passed?' he asked.

'No, you haven't!' said Akela firmly. 'I won't pass you for your Cub Cyclist Badge when half the time you chug down the road going, "Brmm, brmm, brmm, brmm, brmmm!" What do you think you are, a racing-car?'

Nobby shrugged his shoulders.

'I'll give you another test next week,' went on Akela, 'but don't move off yet. I want a word with you after I've seen the other Cubs!'

Akela walked back to the corner to watch the other Cubs come in. Snowy parked his cycle against the kerb.

'Hard luck, Nobby. You'll pass next time.'

'Hope so, Snowy. I've got to learn how to keep my mouth shut first.'

'Don't worry about that now. I want to look in that antique dealer's window. Dad asked me to keep my eyes open for old sports' trophies and medals. He's collecting them. He says they'll become a real part of sports' history and they'll become more and more valuable as time goes on. I always keep my eyes open for cups, sports' medals and badges.'

'I like badges,' said Nobby glumly, 'especially Cyclist Badges.'

The Cubs peered in the antique shop window.

'Can you see any sports' trophies, Nobby?' asked Snowy.

Nobby looked all over.

'What a lot of old junk!' he said. 'Who would ever want to buy that old candle-stick?'

'There's a medal,' shouted Snowy, pointing to a silver coloured disc, the size of a fifty pence piece. 'See that black, Chinese casket full of trinkets and jewellery? Next to it . . . at the back.'

Nobby followed Snowy's directions until he was looking at the medal. Embossed on the face was a figure of a runner.

'L.A.A.C!' he said, reading the letters on the medal. 'What does that mean – Last athlete's a cissy?'

'Lancashire Amateur Athletic Club,' said Snowy. 'That's a good old sports' club. Let's go in and find out how much it is.'

The Cubs went through the door into the over-crowded shop. There they had the greatest difficulty in moving between the tables, sideboards, chests and other furniture which cluttered the place. Inside the shop were two other customers, a lady in a hat piled high with imitation fruit, and a very big woman in a sheepskin coat. There was hardly room to move. The shop was so crowded it was difficult to turn round without knocking over something or other.

The silver-haired antique dealer seemed to belong to the place. He was little, old, even quaint, but he had a certain charm and gentleness. He peered over his

old-fashioned spectacles at a penny-farthing bicycle
leaning against the white-washed wall behind the
counter.

'A hundred and forty pounds, you say?' said the
sweet old lady with the fruit salad hat. 'Is it roadworthy?'

'Roadworthy, madam?' said the little old man.
'Why, you could wheel it straight out of this shop and
ride round the town on it. My grandson gave it a
good overhaul when it came in.'

'Um!' said the fruit salad lady. She was obviously
interested in the machine.

'It's a sturdy bit of work,' went on the antique
dealer. 'Real Victorian. It was built in Birmingham
in eighteen seventy-eight – need I say more? You

can have it for one hundred and forty pounds!'

'One hundred and forty pounds! Um! Would you mind getting it out for me so I can look at it?'

'You want it out, madam? Outside the shop?'

It was difficult to know whether the antique dealer was happy or sad. Certainly he must have wanted to sell the machine, for that was his business. However, there was no doubt that in the crowded shop, it would be extremely inconvenient to wheel it out. Nevertheless, with a bit of puffing and panting, and a lot of manoeuvring, he managed to push the machine from behind the counter.

'Phew!' he puffed. 'I'll wheel it outside the shop and you can have a good look at it.'

The other customer in the shop, the huge woman in the sheepskin coat, almost squashed Nobby against a grandfather clock as she stepped back to make a clear way for the penny-farthing. Miraculously, not an item was knocked over as the antique dealer manoeuvred the machine outside. Snowy watched him through the window, from inside the shop.

'There you are, madam,' said the antique dealer, 'in perfect roadworthy condition. You can see the oil on the bearings. If you like, you can hop on it and give it a try.'

'I don't really think I could ride it,' said the lady, adjusting her fruit laden hat. 'My cycling days are

over, but I really would like to have a demonstration.
Do you think you could give me a demonstration?'

'Me, madam? I'm afraid my riding days are over.
My wind, you know, I've lost my wind.'

'Oh, dear!' The lady looked disappointed. 'I shall
never know if it goes or not, shall I?'

'Just a minute,' said the antique dealer. He called
to Akela who was counting up the names in his note
pad. 'Young man, would you ride a penny-farthing for
this lady? She'd like a demonstration, but I can't ride
now. You can try it out in the cul-de-sac around the
corner. It's quite quiet there.'

'My, this is a beautiful bit of machinery, isn't it?'
said Akela, testing the brakes. 'Okay, mister, I'll give
it a try out for you. I haven't ridden a penny-farthing
before, but I'll give it a try.'

Akela pushed the cycle out of sight, around the
corner.

'Akela's going to ride a penny-farthing,' shrieked
Nobby, from inside the shop. 'Come on, Snowy, let's
go and see him fall off.'

Nobby pushed by the big mountain of a woman and
dashed out of the shop. Snowy went after him.

Quite a crowd had gathered in the side street to
watch the demonstration. Besides the antique dealer
and his customer – the lady in the fruit salad hat – and
the Cubs and marshals from the 2nd Billington Troop,

there was a window-cleaner, a breadman and many shoppers. Snowy had to squeeze through the crowd to see at all. He joined Nobby as Akela leaned the bicycle against a lamp-post. Akela climbed up the lamp-post to seat himself in the saddle.

'How do I start?' asked Akela.

'Pedal the wheels, how do you think?' yelled Nobby. 'Here, I'll show you.'

But Nobby was pushed back by the crowd. Akela took a deep breath and pushed himself away from the lamp-post.

'Keep up your speed, otherwise you'll fall off,' shouted the antique dealer.

Akela wobbled a little, but he soon got the hang of it. He gave, in fact, a remarkable demonstration of

penny-farthing riding. He rode confidently, at a good, steady speed. He gave all the correct hand signals. He turned smoothly at the bottom of the street, and rode back, tooting his horn.

'How do I stop?' he yelled.

'Fall off, fall off, that's your only hope,' called Nobby, as his cap was pushed over his eyes by the surging crowd.

Akela steered the bicycle towards his lamp-post, and as he drew alongside, he jammed on his brakes, then he grabbed the lamp-post before he heeled over. The crowd cheered. Akela climbed down to the ground.

'It's a good bike,' he said, breathlessly. 'It's much smoother than I expected. A good runner.'

'There you are, madam,' said the antique dealer. 'Yours for one hundred and forty pounds – a perfect bargain. It's a good investment, you can sell it again anytime and not lose a penny.'

The old lady was doubtful. 'I'm afraid it's not what I want.'

'What do you want?' said the antique dealer, somewhat surprised. 'What's wrong with it? Listen madam, you can have it for a hundred and thirty-five. I'm offering it to you at a give-away price, because it's taking up too much room in my shop.'

'No, thank you,' said the lady, curtly, then off she trotted down the high street.

'Blimey!' gasped the antique dealer. 'What does she want – gold plating?'

He pushed his cycle back into the shop. The big woman had already left, so it was somewhat easier for him to manoeuvre it between the crowded furniture, and park it behind the counter against the wall.

'Phew!' he said, mopping his brow. He sat on his little stool behind the counter and looked over at Nobby. 'Now what do you want, lad?'

'Nothing,' said Nobby.

'Nothing? What are you doing here?'

'He's with me,' butted in Snowy. 'May I look at that Lancashire Amateur Athletic Club medal? It's in the window next to a black, Chinese casket.'

'The Lancs medal, eh?' The antique dealer smiled, hobbled across to the window and looked around. 'Let me see, where did I put it?'

'Beside the black, Chinese casket,' Snowy repeated.

'Yes, on the second shelf.'

In the window, Snowy could see the sports' medal, but the Chinese casket had gone. The antique dealer looked around.

'Where's the Chinese casket?' he said.

'It . . . it was there, beside the medal, only a few minutes ago,' said Snowy.

'Well, it's not there now,' the antique dealer growled, looking at the Cubs. 'Somebody's taken it.'

'It . . . it wasn't me,' said Nobby. 'I wouldn't have that box of beads if you gave it to me.'

'None of the contents was worth more than two pounds a piece, but that box of beads, as you call it, is worth over five hundred pounds.' The antique dealer shrugged his shoulders as he resigned himself to his loss. He gave Snowy the medal. 'That's twenty pence, son,' he said.

Snowy looked at the medal, and checked that it was not damaged in any way.

'Will you keep it for me, 'til I go home and get some money?'

The antique dealer nodded. 'It will still be here when you come back, that is if no one steals it in the meantime.'

'Thanks,' said Snowy. 'I'll be back as soon as I can.'

With that, Snowy and Nobby left the shop. Akela caught them as they got on their cycles.

'You've passed your cycling test, Snowy,' he said, 'but you should have that seat raised a little. You're a growing boy now. As for you, Nobby, I'm sorry I can't pass you this time, but I'll give you a check next Saturday. Bring your bike along about half past nine, and I'll also show you how to check that it's fully roadworthy, and that includes brakes, tyres, bearings, lights, everything. I'll give it a complete overhaul for you, right?'

Nobby nodded. 'Oh, thanks.'

'I'll see you off then. You're off home, now?'

Snowy nodded. 'Yes, straight down the high street.'

'Right, take care. I'll see you off.'

Akela watched them cycle off safely. Snowy was anxious to get home to collect the twenty pence he needed for the sports' medal, but he had to stop at the level crossing to wait for a passenger train to go through. The train, a diesel for Birmingham, was at the station. As Snowy waited, he watched the passengers board. He saw the woman in the fruit salad hat, and the big woman in the sheepskin coat, behind her, climb into the same compartment. The carriage doors were closed, the train hooted and moved on. When it was clear of the level crossing the gates swung open and the road traffic moved on its way.

Snowy rode on behind Nobby, but now his mind was troubled. He could not imagine why the lady who wanted the penny-farthing bicycle should suddenly change her mind after a faultless demonstration of cycling by Akela. He could not see why the big woman in the sheepskin coat should leave the shop before being served. He could not see why the two women, who had not spoken a word to each other in the shop should travel in the same railway compartment. Suddenly he was suspicious. Perhaps the fruit salad lady had coaxed the antique dealer outside, to leave her accomplice, the big woman, free to help herself . . . Oh, it was so obvious, and so clever, and now those female confidence tricksters had got clean away.

Snowy slowed down and called out to Nobby ahead.

'Just a minute, Nobby. I want to go back to check something.'

'What do you want to check, Snowy? Hey, wait for me!'

Snowy turned off, to double back to the railway station, with Nobby trying to catch up behind. When they got there, Snowy dashed up to the ticket collector.

'Can you remember a lady with lots of artificial fruit on her hat, going on the last Birmingham train?' he asked. 'Please I must know.'

'She was only going as far as Lockingham,'

'And the big woman with her, was she going to Lockingham, too? We think they stole something from the antique dealer's on the corner.'

'Did they now? They didn't look like thieves to me. but you can't tell these days.'

'What time will the train arrive at Lockingham?'

The ticket collector casually looked at his time-table.

'Lockingham. That's about thirty kilometres up the line to Birmingham. Let me see, eleven forty-seven.'

'Eleven forty-seven! Thanks,' said Snowy. 'Eleven forty seven. Eleven forty-seven.'

Snowy dashed out with Nobby trailing behind him, and barged into the antique dealer's shop.

'Come for your medal, have you?' said the antique dealer, getting it out for him.

'No. I think I know who took your Chinese casket,' said Snowy. 'I think two women, the big one and the little one, were confidence tricksters. I think one of them deliberately got you outside, so the other one could rifle the shop.'

The antique dealer put the medal on the counter.

'I came to that conclusion myself, lad,' he said.

'That's an old trick, so old it's obvious. Obvious, yes, so obvious that I didn't realise it was being played on me. Ah, well, there's no fool like an old fool. I've lost five hundred pounds, it could have been more.'

'But . . . but you can't let them get clean away with it!' said Snowy. 'You've . . . someone's got to stop them before they trick someone else.'

'Stop 'em?' The antique dealer laughed. 'I've already given their description to the police, but even the police can't stop them. They could be miles away by now, anywhere.'

'They're on the Birmingham train,' said Snowy. 'I saw them get on, in the same compartment. I checked and found they had tickets for Lockingham. They will get off the train at Lockingham at eleven forty-seven.'

The antique dealer's eyes sparkled behind his spectacles.

'Are you sure?'

Snowy nodded. 'Positive. I checked.'

The antique dealer hurried to the telephone and called the police.

' . . . yes, eleven forty-seven at Lockingham, off the Birmingham train . . .'

When finally he put down the telephone, he turned to the Cubs.

'I hope you get it back,' said Snowy.

'I'll keep my fingers crossed.'

Snowy turned to leave.

'Here,' said the antique dealer. 'You've forgotten your medal.'

'I . . . I haven't been home for my money, yet,' said Snowy.

The antique dealer held out the medal.

'There'll be no charge this time, son.' But before he handed it over, he had another good look at it. There was a far away look in his eyes. 'Aye, this medal takes me back a few years. I got it running from Preston to Blackpool in nineteen twenty-six, it must have been. It's almost an antique now.' He handed Snowy the medal. 'I . . . the old athlete who won it would like you to have it.'

'Thank you very much,' said Snowy, rubbing the medal on his sleeve to give it a polish. 'I'll take great care of it, always, I promise.'

'I'm sure you will,' said the antique dealer. 'You look a smart lad to me. I'm pleased someone will look after it when I've gone. And,' he added as an afterthought, 'if I do get back my Chinese casket, I'll have another little present for you.'

And that was how Snowy won an Olympic Bronze medal for his Dad's collection.

7 · Prize steer

The next Saturday was an outstanding day. It was
Snowy's mother's birthday. It was the day Sunder-
land won the F.A. Cup. It was the day Akela heard
he had got through his engineering examinations. And
it was the day Nobby passed his cycling test. Nobby
passed his cycling test! True, he passed his cycling
test!

Akela had got Nobby to bring his cycle round for
the test in the morning, and he asked Snowy to come
along and help. First of all, Akela thoroughly checked
the bicycle for roadworthiness, then he explained
exactly what he wanted Nobby to do. Then he set
Nobby off on his test around the quiet backstreets.

Nobby was a gawky rider, (but he is also a gawky
walker, a gawky talker, a gawky eater – and
nothing in the world can change that now). But
Nobby was not a show-off. He didn't ride dangerously,
or without consideration for other road users. He was
not selfish or bad-tempered. Unlike Snowy, he did not

ride smooth, fast and well, but like Snowy, he rode safely. Akela did not show him any favouritism. Nobby kept his mouth shut and passed his cycling test!

'You've passed,' said Akela, as if he couldn't believe his own words. He pulled himself together. 'Mind you, that doesn't mean to say that you can take things easy from now on, or that cycling with the Cyclist Badge is any easier than cycling without one. Everyday, that is today, tomorrow and every other day, you must always make sure you ride safely. Accidents happen to experienced riders as well as any others, so make sure it doesn't happen to you. You know my saying – it's better to be five minutes late for your appointment that fifty years early for your funeral. Understand?'

Nobby nodded. He understood.

'Right. You can go home for your lunch now, and be back at Cub Headquarters at two for our nature study expedition to Evensdon Woods.'

'May we go on our bikes, honk, honk, honk?' said Nobby.

'Ah, but . . .' said Akela. Now he was stuck for words. 'It's . . . it's a fair way.'

'It's only ten minutes down Evensdon Lane,' said Snowy.

'Honk, honk, honk!' said Nobby.

'Stop that horrible honking noise,' said Akela. He pondered for a moment. 'All right, all right. You two can go on your bikes, provided you both get written permission from your parents. If you don't, I'll meet you at Cub Headquarters at two and you'll go by mini-bus with the rest of us, understand?'

'Message received and understood,' said Nobby, rubbing his hands.

So in the afternoon, Snowy and Nobby, each with a note from his parents in his pocket, rode off down Evensdon Lane for Evensdon Woods.

'We'll ride single file,' said Snowy, 'to leave more room for overtaking traffic.'

'Right,' said Nobby, keeping his eyes on the road.

Akela's talks, lectures and stories and demonstrations on road safety during the past few months obviously had a remarkable effect on the riding ability of his Cubs. Nobby rode his bicycle in a manner which could only be described as sensible. He kept up a steady speed, but he slowed and stopped in good time at red or amber traffic lights, and he was ready to move on again as soon as they changed to green. He gave all the correct signals, and never once was Snowy, behind, in any doubt as to what he was going to do. He was courtesy itself. It was a pleasure to be on the roads with him

Just after they got onto the straight, the Scout

mini-bus, loaded with Cubs, overtook them. Akela pipped his horn, the Cubs shouted greetings and parted. In a few minutes, they would all meet up again for their nature study expedition – or so they thought!

Snowy and Nobby rode on. It was not a particularly bright day, but there was not much traffic on the road. Nobby confidently led the way. Snowy was not far behind, but their luck was not to last. Nobby turned round a corner, honked wildly and yelled out in alarm. Snowy came round the corner just in time to see Nobby run straight into a young steer, blocking

the narrow lane. The accident was unavoidable. Nobby skidded straight into the animal, and shot, not only over his handlebars, but over the steer's back.

Snowy braked just in time. He stopped his bicycle and propped it against the hawthorn hedge.

'Are you all right, Nobby?'

Nobby crawled away on the other side of the steer as fast as he could.

'What's that nelephant doing in the middle of the road?' he said.

He shook his head. He was unhurt.

Snowy advanced, picked up Nobby's bicycle and put it out of harm's way next to his. The steer lowered it's head, but was too afraid to charge.

'It must have escaped,' said Nobby.

Snowy nodded. 'We've got to get it off the road before it causes an accident.'

'It's already caused an accident,' said Nobby, rubbing his head.

'Let's move it off the road,' said Snowy. 'There must be a gate somewhere down this lane. We can turn it into a field, where it can stay until we get help. Come on, Nobby.'

Snowy advanced on the young steer, which turned and ambled down the country lane. All the time, Snowy kept his eyes open for a gate leading into a field, where he could leave the steer safely. He never realised he could walk so far without seeing a farm-yard gate. In fact, the first gate he saw was one which led into the yard of the local horse-riding school. Snowy made a quick decision. He decided the steer would be safer in the riding school than on the road.

'Stay behind the steer,' said Snowy, running past the animal. 'We'll move it into the riding school.'

The Cubs ushered the steer into the yard quite successfully.

'Where shall we put it now?' asked Nobby.

'Put it in the stables. Open the door, will you?'

Nobby opened the half doors of a stable and Snowy manoeuvred in the steer. The animal seemed quite content, for it nibbled at the hay in the manger.

'What will happen if one of the riders comes in for a ride,' said Nobby, 'saddles up that thing and tries to trot off for a ride across country?'

'I don't know about that,' said Snowy, 'but we've got to let someone know we've got a steer locked up. We ought to telephone the police. I wonder where the nearest telephone is?'

'I know!' Nobby snapped his fingers. 'If we follow the telegraph wires along the side of the road, they'll lead us to a telephone.

'Good idea! We'll try that,' said Snowy.

But just as the Cubs set off down the lane, they

looked back and saw the horse riding party turning into the gate.

'Double back, Nobby. One of the riders is bound to know where a telephone is.'

The Cubs dashed back to the stables, and caught up with the riders just as they were dismounting outside. The young steer looked out over the half door. One little girl on a pony, looked at it in amazement. She rubbed her eyes.

'Mith Mitchell, that pony hath horns,' she lisped.

The riding mistress looked up.

'That's a steer,' explained Snowy.

'A steer!' said the riding mistress. 'What's a steer doing in my stables?'

'Having a good feed when I last saw it,' said Nobby.

'We found the steer in the lane,' explained Snowy. 'We moved it here so it would not cause an accident. I hope you don't mind. When I can find a telephone, I'll contact the police and they can find out who's it is.'

'The police were looking for a young steer back at the cross roads,' said another rider. 'They asked me if I'd seen it.'

'Ah, so that's it?' said the riding mistress, looking at the steer. 'There's a telephone in my office. I'll give the police a ring.'

'Oh, thanks,' said Snowy. 'If we can leave it to you

now, we'd like to go. We're late for a Cub Scout meeting.'

'Yes, yes, of course. There's nothing to worry about now,' said the riding mistress. 'By the way, what's your name?'

'Snowy.'

'Snowy! What a delightful name. It is a nice name, isn't it? I have awful trouble thinking up names for my ponies. Snowy is a nice name. If ever I get a white pony, I shall call him Snowy. The trouble is, white ponies are so expensive, for me anyway.'

Nobby groaned, as Snowy shuffled uneasily. The riding mistress was perfectly free to call her ponies whatever she wished, but he wasn't at all happy about her using his name.

'Why not call him Starlight?' suggested Snowy instead.

'That's another nice name,' said the riding mistress.

'What's your name?' she asked Nobby.

'Nobby!' croaked Nobby, as gruffly as he could. 'It's a rotten name for a horse.'

'I couldn't agree with you more,' said the riding mistress. 'I wouldn't be seen dead riding a horse named Nobby.'

Nobby heaved a sigh of relief.

'Snowy and Nobby,' repeated the riding mistress, looking at the shoulder badges of the Cubs, 'of the

2nd Billington Cub Scout Pack, that's right, isn't it?'

Snowy nodded.

'Right, I'll tell the police if they want to know, and I'll look after the animal until the farmer comes to collect it.'

'Thank you very much,' said Snowy. He took Nobby by the arm. 'Let's go!' he said quickly.

As soon as the Cubs were outside the gates, Nobby groaned.

'Isn't it awful?' he said.

'What's awful?' said Snowy.

'She wanted to use your name for a pony. She's got a cheek, hasn't she?'

'I don't think she ever will,' said Snowy. 'You heard her say white ponies are too expensive for her.'

'But she might!'

Snowy swallowed his pride. 'Anyway I don't care what she calls it. The point is, we'd better get a move on, otherwise Akela will be after us.'

The Cubs collected their bicycles and met Akela, who had come back to look for them. At first Akela, was angry with them for going astray but after he had heard their explanations, he agreed that they had behaved in a true Cub Scout manner. Still, they had a busy afternoon's programme ahead of them, and Akela was anxious to waste no more time. When at last he collected all his Cubs together, he led them on their expedition in the woods.

The Cubs had a busy afternoon, and returned home well satisfied with themselves. Snowy and Nobby returned together, and when they approached Nobby's house, they saw Mr Clark burning the weeds off his path with a flame thrower. Mrs Clark was leaning over the gate talking to a neighbour.

'Hey, where have you been?' she said to Nobby. 'Don't you know the tv men have been looking for you? Said something about a lost steer. You haven't been letting any animals out of their fields, have you?

'No, no,' said Nobby. 'We found one in the middle of the lane, that's all. It was only a little one.'

Mrs Clark turned back to her neighbour.

'Gave me a turn, they did, arriving here with their vans and cameras. Thought they were going to film a bull-fight or something.'

'It might be on the local tv news,' said Snowy.

'Us, you mean?' asked Nobby.

'No, the lost steer. It may be very valuable.'

Nobby frowned. 'Maybe there's a reward. Maybe the tv people wanted to find us to give us the reward for finding a very valuable animal.'

Snowy shrugged his shoulder. That sounded like wishful thinking to him. But Nobby was really excited.

'Let's go in and watch tv' he said. 'Is it all right if we go in and watch tv, Dad?'

'Take your dirty boots off.'

'Thanks, Dad.'

Snowy and Nobby went into the house and Nobby plugged in the tv set. The programme showed experts discussing the afternoon's cup final match, which would have interested Snowy had he been able to watch it, but what upset Nobby were the recollections of their afternoon's escapade.

'What would you do if they really called a pony Snowy?' said Nobby, still upset that his pal should be so awfully treated.

'Doesn't worry me!' said Snowy, firmly.

'Ah, Snowy, it's not right.'

Eventually, the local news came on, and sure enough, there was an account of how a farmer had bought and lost a prize steer. The cameras showed the riding mistress telling how the steer had been rounded up by two local Cubs called Snowy and Nobby. The farmer himself was very relieved that his valuable animal had been recovered, for it was a special breed which had cost him a lot of money on that very same day.

The cameras also showed the contented animal looking out of the horse stables.

'And what do you call this fine animal?' asked the tv news man.

'I haven't given him a name yet,' said the farmer. 'Not yet, I'll have to think of one . . . '

The little horsey girl in the crowd shouted out, 'Why not call him Nobby?'

The farmer smiled. 'Good idea! Why not? After the clever little boy who found him. Aye! I will.'

The film ended with a shot of 'Nobby' being led out of the stable yard to a waiting cattle truck.

For a moment the real Nobby was speechless, then he threw his cap at the tv set. Snowy clenched his teeth. He realised how embarrassed his pal was.

'Er . . . fine animal.' Snowy said. 'Er . . . it should win lots of prizes at shows. It's . . . it's a champion.'

'Huh!' said Nobby in disgust. 'It may be a champion, but that's no reason why it should be called after me. I shouldn't have told that riding mistress my name was Nobby.'

'But she did ask you your name,' said Snowy. 'What . . . what else could you have said?'

'Rhubarb!' said Nobby.

More Beaver Books

On the following pages you will find some other exciting Beaver Books to look out for in your local bookshop

MIDNIGHT ADVENTURE

Written and illustrated by Raymond Briggs

Gerry and Tim are planning a midnight fishing expedition. All the details have been minutely worked out and the two boys can hardly wait to set off. But when they get to the lake on the golf course, it's not quite how they imagined. There are lots of creepy noises and they feel very alone.

Their suspicions are aroused when a lorry drives past them with its lights and engine switched off. It is heading for the golf club . . .

Gerry and Tim decide to investigate and there starts the adventure of a lifetime.

THE STRANGE HOUSE

Written and illustrated by Raymond Briggs

Tim and Gerry knew they should not be on the golf course. Running away from some angry golfers, they found themselves in the grounds of a strange house. Why is the house boarded up? Why does the fierce woman try to chase them away? And whose is the mysterious facc at an upstairs window? The only way Tim and Gerry can find out is to get into the house . . . somehow . . .

EMIL AND HIS CLEVER PIG

Astrid Lindgren

Emil, the naughty little Swedish boy, is up to mischief again!
First he paints his sister blue, then he sets fire to the parson's
wife, and then he locks his father in the lavatory! And on
Tuesday the tenth of August, he does something so bad that
his mother won't even write about it in the blue exercise book
(but *you* read about it here).

THE SIEGE OF COBB STREET SCHOOL

Hazel Townson

When gunmen burst in and hold their class hostage, Lenny and Jake are hiding in the cloakroom having a sneaky bag of crisps — and that's how they manage to escape.

But what are they to do? Will they be able to get in touch with people outside the school to warn them of what is happening? Can they outwit the gunmen and rescue their friends?

'Told with great gusto and will delight readers of primary school age who like plenty of action' *Junior Bookshelf*

URSULA BEAR

Sheila Lavelle

Ursula likes bears – big bears, little bears, fat bears, thin bears, in fact, any kind of bears. So when she finds a magic spell to turn a little girl into a bear, she is thrilled to bits!

And when the circus comes to town, and she can't afford a ticket, turning herself into a bear seems to be a very good idea. The trouble is, things are never quite as simple as they seem . . .

If you're an eager Beaver reader, perhaps you ought to try some more of our exciting titles. They are available in bookshops or they can be ordered directly from us. Just complete the form below and enclose the right amount of money and the books will be sent to you at home.

☐	HELLO MR TWIDDLE	Enid Blyton	85p
☐	THE ENCHANTED WOOD	Enid Blyton	95p
☐	THE MAGIC FARAWAY TREE	Enid Blyton	95p
☐	HEIDI'S SONG		95p
☐	URSULA BEAR	Sheila Lavelle	75p
☐	NICHOLAS ON HOLIDAY	Goscinny and Sempé	95p
☐	EMIL IN THE SOUP TUREEN	Astrid Lindgren	95p
☐	LOLLIPOP	Christine Nostlinger	£1.25
☐	THE WORST KIDS IN THE WORLD	Barbara Robinson	95p
☐	THE BROWNIES IN HOSPITAL	Pamela Sykes	95p
☐	THE GREAT ICE CREAM CRIME	Hazel Townson	85p
☐	THE MILL HOUSE CAT	Marjorie Ann Watts	£1.00
☐	BOGWOPPIT	Ursula Moray Williams	95p

And if you would like to hear more about Beaver Books, and find out all the latest news, don't forget the BEAVER BULLETIN. Just send a stamped, self-addressed envelope to Beaver Books, 17-21 Conway Street, London W1P 6JD.

If you would like to order books, please send this form, and the money due to:

HAMLYN PAPERBACK CASH SALES, PO BOX 11, FALMOUTH, CORNWALL TR10 9EN.

Send a cheque or postal order, and don't forget to include postage at the following rates: UK: 55p for first book, 22p for the second, 14p thereafter; BFPO and Eire: 55p for first book, 22p for the second, 14p per copy for next 7 books, 8p per book thereafter; Overseas £1.00 for first book, 25p thereafter.

NAME..

ADDRESS...

....

Please print clearly